MURDERHOUSE

MURDERHOUSE

A

NOVELIZATION

PUPPET COMBO®

+

REGINA WATTS

© 2021 Vague Scenario LLC
ISBN: 978-1-7359008-5-8

All rights reserved. No part of this book may be reproduced or transmitted in any form or by any means, including mechanical, electronic, photocopying, recording or otherwise, without the express written consent of Vague Scenario LLC.

Concept & Original Game: Vague Scenario LLC
Text: Regina Watts
Editing: Sydney Sowers
Typesetting: M. F. Sullivan
Cover: Patrick Driscoll

Puppet Combo® Online: https://puppetcombo.com
Regina Watts Online: https://www.hrhdegenetrix.com

PROLOGUE

1985

THE RABBIT'S VACANT eyes fixed on Justin.

Hand tightening in his mother's grip, the boy recoiled. Ahead of them, the line surged forward with one rippling centipede step.

"Say 'Cheese,'" urged the photographer.

Justin stared up at his mother. She smiled as she continued rattling off relatives deserving of a photographic print that Easter. While the camera snapped and immortalized another child, she said, "Oh—and Aunt Bernadette! We can't forget her... hm..."

She tapped her chin.

"Maybe we should sign up for that package they offer."

"Mom."

"Your father was annoyed at me when I brought it home last year, but what good is just *one* photograph, anyway?"

"Mom?"

"I mean—the copies your father made of your Christmas photos were so crummy, and—"

"*Mom!*"

Justin's mother finally glanced down at him. Her big, slightly wet eyes batted with a single mascara-spiked blink.

"Yes, sweetie?"

"Mom," he said, "I don't really want to do this."

"Oh, honey." Laughing, squeezing his hand, Justin's mom stepped forward in line and forced him to shuffle up alongside her. "There's no reason to be nervous!"

"The rabbit is staring at me."

"Hm?"

A slight furrow touched her brow. Justin recognized it from when he recounted a nightmare or tried to get her to believe that sometimes the shadows moved in his bedroom at night.

Now she looked over at the rabbit, whose dusky pink fur brightened under the brilliant illumination of a flashbulb.

Justin couldn't stand to look with her. He avidly studied the blue toes of his sneakers while his mother said in a merry way, "Now, I think he's cute! Come on, Justin. You used to love getting your picture taken with the Easter Bunny. What happened?"

What happened? Maybe that was a better question for the mall. Justin tried to remember what it had been like on previous occasions when his mother had forced him to undergo this strange holiday ritual.

In his naïve memory, the bunny was so bright and innocent.

Had it always looked this way? Had it always had such huge black pits for eyes? Had its fur always been such a sickly, faded hue?

Had its head turned a little more all the time to keep its empty eyes fixed on Justin?

"I just don't want to do this," Justin said, looking frantically toward the throng of people flowing through the vast halls of the eerie mall.

Amid the sheer scale of the architecture and the conversations of the shoppers and the shrieks of happier children and the photographer's constant recitation of the mantra, "Next," the too-cheerful melody of "Peter Cottontail" was almost entirely drowned.

Almost.

"Honey! There's nothing to be afraid of."

"I'm not afraid," Justin lied reflexively, no more able to confess to fear than was any other boy his age. "I just don't want to. It's babyish."

"But you're *my* baby."

"I'm eight," he corrected her tersely, counting the number of people ahead of them.

Four people. Four families with four kids. That was still enough time to change his mother's mind.

"Look! All these kids are little."

"That boy back there looks *older* than you."

Seeing his posture was no more agreeable than it had been before, his mother frowned and released his hand.

Justin's first impulse was to run, but then she would know he was afraid.

And anyway—anyway, he was being ridiculous.

Here he was complaining about babies when he was *acting* like a baby!

Justin turned this paradox over as much as his young mind would allow while his mother laid on a guilt-trip second to none.

"You're growing up so fast, Justin," she said, staring earnestly into his eyes. "It's so special to see you grow every day into a wonderful, smart, funny young man—but it's a little sad, too."

The camera's shutter snapped. Its flash bulb cracked like lightning.

Everything was illuminated but the rabbit's black eyes.

"I know you're ready to be an adult as soon as possible," his mother summarized. Justin forced himself to focus on her. "But you'll only be a kid once… and the opportunities to see you being a kid, they're getting fewer and fewer."

"Next!"

Justin glanced again toward the crowd of freer shoppers while his oblivious mother said, "I want to seize these moments while I still can. I want to be able to look back one day and say that nothing was wasted—that I took every opportunity I could to be *present* in your childhood while it was happening. Maybe you'll only understand what I mean when you're older, but…"

Her eyes glassed with tears.

Justin exhaled in a mingling of emotions: sorrow of his own, plus an indefinable background emotion that was something close to frustration.

Frustration, and—yes.

Maybe fear.

"Peter Cottontail" was louder near the gazebo

where the rabbit posed for photos. As a girl a couple years younger than Justin perched upon its knee and smiled up into its soulless face, Justin wondered what it was that made it so easy for other kids to do this. Maybe he really *was* scared—just a big scaredy-cat.

And because Justin was a big scaredy-cat, his mother was upset.

He had to be brave for his mother.

"No, Mom," said Justin, puffing out his chest and shifting back his shoulders. "I'll do it."

The tears disappeared at once. Her face expanded into a radiant smile that filled Justin with relief as much as with pride. Another emotional crisis averted.

"Thank you so much, sweetie. Don't worry...I won't make you do anything like this next year if you really don't want to. Just—let's have this one last picture, okay?"

Okay.

Okay.

The father and son ahead of them whispered to one another while the photograph snapped the current subject. Justin was a close study of the natural way the girl hugged the bunny, then slid off its knee and bounced to her waiting mother.

"Next!"

The line surged forward.

Without warning, the father and son ahead of them left the line.

Justin balked, his palms wet with sweat. As he wiped them off on his denim shorts and then, finding that insufficient, on the neon yellow fabric of his t-shirt, his mother watched the other two go and said in a soft murmur, "See? You're not the only nervous one."

"I'm not," Justin muttered at the scuffed floor while the next photo was posed. "Not—nervous."

"Of course not, honey," said his mother with a fond smile and a ruffle of his black hair.

While he reached up with a frown and fixed what she'd mussed, she made a noise of delight to see the bulb go off.

"Here we go! It'll all be over soon, sweetie. Just grin and bear it. Maybe the Easter Bunny will leave some extra chocolates in your basket since he saw you in person!"

This Easter Bunny coming to his house while he slept? Justin's blood ran cold.

The child upon its knee bounced to their parent.

Justin's hands clenched in fists at his sides.

Somebody said something he didn't hear while he fortified his nerves.

"Honey," his mother said.

"*Next*," the photographer repeated.

Justin came back to Earth to find the man staring daggers at him.

The rabbit stared, too.

The hollows of its socket-like eyes seemed to somehow grow larger.

Suddenly, Justin found his legs no longer worked.

"Come on, kid! Look at that line, we don't have all day."

"Go on, honey."

His mother's manicured hands fit to his slim shoulders. She squeezed a bit, pushing him until he stumbled forward. His other leg caught up with him and he made himself progress another step.

Another.

"Go on," said the photographer under his breath

when Justin was close enough to hear, "get your ass up there."

Justin took a deep breath.

The empty-eyed rabbit sat upon a white wicker throne, the gazebo around it like some perverse cage. Justin couldn't explain why he hated the flat blue backdrop's effect, but it made him think of the science fiction stories his father read to him sometimes. It was like the rabbit existed in another dimension. Like it and its chair were on the other side of a doorway to a place Justin didn't want to know about.

"Don't keep the nice man waiting, sweetie," his mother implored, the slightly nervous tone peaking her voice.

Exhaling, Justin climbed the short set of stairs to the platform where the Easter Bunny waited for him.

The reek made him stop short again.

Justin's breath hitched. He stared into the soulless face of the Easter Bunny and remembered the time when he and his mother were at the drugstore. A homeless man had come in to pay for cigarettes in loose change and crumpled dollars, and Justin had been surprised at the time by the intensity of the smell.

Then, it had made him sad.

Now, it made him afraid.

The scent of a hard life and poverty became the stench of rank death when it exuded from the Easter Bunny's patchy fur. It made Justin drop from his mind all childish pretense.

Suddenly it was evident that this was *not* the Easter Bunny. This was a person in a costume. A grown man in a bunny costume with lifeless, hateful eyes.

A man who breathed heavily, as Justin forced

himself to slowly perch upon the edge of the rabbit's threadbare knee.

The breath was all Justin could hear.

"Peter Cottontail" faded into the background.

So did the sound of the mall's clamor or the frantic timpani of his own heart.

So did the photographer's command, "Smile, kid!"

All Justin could hear was the breath.

The heaving, somehow ragged breath, as though the man in the rabbit costume were trying to keep himself from breathing *too* heavily.

But there it was all the same.

The breaths. The in and out of a lion behind the glass of a zoo.

The rabbit's hand came to rest upon Justin's shoulder.

By the time the flash of the camera resolved, Justin's leap had landed him at the base of the gazebo stairs. As soon as his feet were on the floor, he bolted, unaware of the photographer's profanity or his mother's cry.

He was only aware of the intense animal pressure to get away, get far away.

The rabbit's hand seemed to lay heavily upon his shoulder and the odor pursued him like a shadow. Fists pumping, Justin ducked between shoppers and cut through families. He ran and ran, his heart pounding against his ribs as though it were about to burst.

No matter where he looked, no place was safe. If he hid in a store, his mother would find him and admonish him for not taking the picture. She might even march him back and *make* him take a better one. That really would have been awful: Justin never wanted to see that rabbit again.

No, no way. He had to find a place to hide and figure out how to talk her into taking him straight home. Maybe, when the coast was clear, he could call his father and ask him to put his foot down on Justin's behalf.

Yeah, that was it. That was it. He'd wait until things were calm and call Dad, and Dad would make it right.

At last, Justin saw it. The one safe place: a picture booth whose star-dotted curtain was not just chained but barred with the flap of an OUT OF ORDER sign.

Relief flooding him, Justin flipped the sign up, ducked under the chain, then let the barrier fall back into place behind him while he closed the curtain and caught his breath in the vinyl seat.

"Justin? Justin!"

With surprising haste, his mother's shrill voice cut through the busy noises of the mall.

Justin held his breath, fear racing through him to realize what he'd just done. She must have been chasing him.

Now she was going to be *really* mad.

"Justin!"

The urgency of her voice rose even higher when she repeated his name a little farther down the hall, her voice near enough to the food court that he knew she had missed him.

Justin shut his eyes in relief.

"Justin! Justin, where are you?"

He wanted to go out to her, of course. But, more than that, he wanted her to be reasonable.

And, well…if he went out now, she'd be anything but reasonable.

Yes—he'd have to call his dad just as soon as his

mother was well out of earshot. He'd find a payphone, call collect, and that'd be that. Dad would talk to Mom, Mom would calm down, and Justin wouldn't be in trouble. He'd be understood.

His parents would understand that it wasn't fear to be averse to something evil.

It was just human nature.

1

1988

EMMA TOOK AN envious breath of the freshly brewed coffees she ferried up the elevator to Channel 9's floor. At least she didn't have to take the stairs this time. Smelling the stuff was torture enough...if she managed to burn herself one more time, Emma was going to tell them exactly where they could stick their freaking internship.

Oh...who was she kidding?

It was a dysfunctional station, sure—and she might not have been paid for the time she spent running errands, transmitting messages and acting as an impromptu janitor—but Emma could never quite get Gary's first speech to her out of her head.

"This is a great opportunity for you, kid," he'd said with a clammy shake of her hand. "Don't screw it up."

He was right, she hated to admit. Ever since Chip Winston of Channel 5 was killed on the scene of a news report about five years prior, Channel 9's greatest rival in the Monroe news game had gained a paradoxical increase in popularity. More viewers meant bigger budgets from advertisers, and bigger budgets from advertisers meant paid interns. Paid interns meant application competition—*stiff* competition.

Stiff enough that Emma, despite her glowing recommendations from professors and part-time employers alike, had still somehow been rejected no fewer than three times from the Channel 5 internship program.

That was fine. Everything happened for a reason, it was said. Emma accepted it was her lot in life to spend a few months—maybe even a year—interning at Channel 9 for free.

But she had always had a feeling about Channel 9.

To call it a 'good' feeling would have been very strong. Maybe even incorrect. No: it was a feeling of impending greatness of some kind or another. It was some intuitive nag Emma had when she envisioned her future. It seemed to her that, if she was going to make it into the journalism industry and become the kind of groundbreaking Woodward or Bernstein she'd always dreamed of being, these first steps at Channel 9 were going to be vital.

If she was going to be a great muckraker, Emma was going to have to spend a lot of early time floating in that muck.

If only greatness had anything to do with goodness!

With comfort.

With respect.

"Well, you're going to *have* to touch *a* dog," Gary was in the middle of telling Dana, mopping his bald brow with a handkerchief the same garish pink as his tracksuit. Across from the producer stood Channel 9's most notoriously short-tempered reporter, both hands on her hips and all her slight weight upon one heeled foot—which allowed the other to occasionally tap in irritation.

Ignoring Dana's body language (much as he ignored Emma when she arrived at his pudgy elbow with the coffee he grabbed in automation), Gary continued, "Look, these are—you know, *fancy* dogs. Purebreds! These ain't some mutts from the street, Dana, baby. They got papers."

"I told you last *week*, Gary. I *don't like dogs*!"

Briskly glancing toward Emma as she snatched a coffee cup from the Styrofoam tray, then once again scrutinizing the line of five happily panting Westminster hopefuls whose owners gossiped in the lights of the set, Dana at least had presence of mind enough to lower her voice.

"Why don't I just sit in a chair off to the side like it's a talk show format?"

"Because the dogs are gonna be walkin' around! They're *show* dogs, Dana, they're meant to be shown—hey!"

Emma had turned to whisk the coffees off to their next stop but paused to look at her boss, hopeful he might have something positive to say for the first time in her three months of thankless toil.

"You drink my second coffee last time, intern?"

"Um—no? I put it on your desk, like—"

"Yeah, well, maybe you misplaced it. It wasn't there after we finished shooting yesterday morning's segment. Pay more attention next time, okay? And get back here once you've done your rounds. I've got a couple of phone calls I need made. Anyway"—just like that, he picked his conversation with Dana right back up and left Emma, face reddened by the insult, standing with her mouth open—"look, Dana, you gotta understand the dilemma! People think you're a *robot*. We need you to seem more personable."

"But I'm *not* personable, Gary."

"That's why you're on thin ice." Emma slipped away, her ears still tuned to the conversation as she scanned for Tom and found him behind the camera. "Just pick a damn dog to pet and film a bumper with it. I don't care which one."

"Good God—fine! Fine, Gary...I guess that poodle looks well-mannered..."

"Hey, Emma." Tom glanced up from the camera with a nod, slipping his headphones from his head and letting them hang around his neck. As she extended the drinks and let herself become deaf to the conversation on the other side of the room, he took a coffee and said, "It's too early in the day for you to look so tired!"

This was one of Tom's favorite comments for her, along with discussions about weather and her family's health. He was a nice enough guy, she guessed; but although he was one of the only employees who talked to her like she was human, Emma couldn't help finding Tom a little dull. He was used to having conversations with his elderly mother, she guessed. Dana had said once that he didn't get out much since he stayed at home to take care of her.

"I try to get to bed early," she settled on telling him, too professionally cautious to reveal the source of her slightly pensive nature in the halls of Channel 9, "but it's hard work keeping Gary off my back all day."

"I'll say. Seems to me like he could learn how to talk to people a little more decently...sometimes I think the channel's doing as badly as it is because of him."

She might not have been willing to add to the gossip pool, but Emma was always glad to listen to existing rumors. "Really? What makes you say that?"

"Who wants to work with a guy like him?" Tom shrugged, taking the lid off his selected coffee cup and snorting an appreciative inhalation of its contents. "I'm sure we've lost more than one interview to his bad attitude...more than one reporter, too. Roberta Taylor over at Channel 5? She used to be one of ours before they needed somebody to replace Chip. I think she must have had her resume in their inbox by the time the sun was up the next day."

Emma laughed and shook her head. "How gross. Did you see they're planning some kind of 5-Year Anniversary thing for him this October?"

"I'll bet they are! It's great ratings. Channel 5 only would have loved it more if he'd been offed on the air...if that had happened, we never would have recovered."

A shudder rolled through Emma. She had been in high school at the time of that particular event. It had a lasting impact on her psyche, along with the psyches of every other citizen of Monroe. Actual footage of a murder would have only made it worse.

"I don't know," Emma said with a frown. "People

like the macabre, but I think most of us draw the line somewhere."

"Don't be so sure…true crime is popular. I just heard Gary and a couple of other producers planning a puff piece about the Easter Ripper the other day… *some* team is going to end up stuck with it. Let's hope it isn't us."

Emma's ears perked. "The Easter Ripper? The guy who got the electric chair last year?"

Tom winced at a hot sip of coffee and set the cup aside to cool. "The crimes are still so fresh, you'd think nobody'd want to touch it…but that's Gary for you. He'll throw out any idea at a pitch meeting, no matter how tasteless."

Shaking her head, Emma opened her mouth to agree but was interrupted by Gary's sharp whistle.

A few of the dogs whipped their heads, the poodle in particular straining on its leash at the sound.

"All right, people," called Gary with a clap of his hands and not the least thought to the effect his call to order had on the very subjects of the piece about to be filmed, "let's get this show on the road! Intern! Quit flirting with Tom."

Scoffing, blushing, Emma exchanged a quick glance of embarrassment with Tom and cleared her throat.

"Catch you later," she said, trying not to sound or look as annoyed as she felt.

"Yeah," was all he said, sliding the headphones up over his ears again.

With a deep breath and an effort to swallow her rage, Emma ditched the Styrofoam carrier in the nearest garbage can and brought the remaining cup to Gary's office down the hall.

What a jerk! Some people just got off on belittling others. Emma knew that, but that didn't make it any less insulting when an abrasive person accused her of something like theft. As if Emma would steal his latte! It probably wasn't even any good.

In the open doorway of Gary's office, Emma looked down at the cup in hesitation. With a glance up and down the hall, then toward the open door through which Dana could be seen beginning her usual patter, Emma slipped into Gary's office and shut the door behind her.

If he really wanted to tell her she was a slacker, maybe she should act like one every once in a while.

As predicted, the latte was subpar and the milk that had been added carried a strange, scalded flavor. Still, it tasted like petty victory. Emma sipped it out of principle while wandering around Gary's office, where the walls bore a panoply of photographs: Gary slightly thinner and graduating from journalism school; Gary shaking hands with President Nixon for who knew what reason; Gary and the daughter he hadn't seen on more than a holiday in something like four years. It was all sort of sad, in a way.

When her wandering ended at the desk, Emma took a peek at the pile of papers there to divine the phone numbers she'd have to call.

Instead she found a file folder labelled MURDER HOUSE PIECE.

Glancing up to the door, Emma set the coffee down and slowly lifted the top flap of the file.

The black eyes of the Easter Ripper's bunny head stared back through time and space, matte even in the gloss of the photo.

Shuddering to see the buck-toothed head

dismembered on a table labeled EVIDENCE, Emma shut the folder and shook her head.

Another puff piece! Always filler with this channel. What there was to be said about the Ripper's killing spree had been said over and over during his rushed capture, trial, and expedited (for the American justice system) trip to the electric chair. It went almost without saying that it was Channel 5, what with their new emphasis on true crime, that did most of the saying.

When would Channel 9 have its moment in the sun? When would they find the piece that rocketed them into validation?

When would *they* break the news?

Leaving the sipped coffee on her boss's desk as she'd been told, Emma meandered from the office and had the door shut behind her just as the barking started.

Dana's outraged scream followed soon after.

"Damn it, Gary! What did I tell you?"

A dog yelped; more dogs barked. Gary's round frame lumbered past the doorway as he called, "Where's that intern? Intern! Intern, grab that poodle!"

Sighing, Emma broke into a sprint.

2

JERRY'S KNUCKLES TIGHTENED on the wheel as he approached the Smith murder house. All traces of early morning exhaustion flew from his mind.

He hated the place and didn't want the first thing to do with it—didn't want the first thing to do with that scummy Channel 9 producer, Gary. But when a man needs money, a man needs money; and money just wasn't in Monroe real estate at that point in time.

So, when that greasy bastard from Channel 9 called Jerry in hopes of sniffing around the murder house and offered to throw in $50, well...it was tempting, though ill-advised.

The last time a piece of real estate owned by Hammer & Croft had appeared in a Channel 9 special, the owners had thrown a big fit. They'd threatened to fire the person who had allowed the televised demonstration of questionable construction—whenever they figured out who that person was.

Fearing for his job, Jerry had told himself he'd put the brakes on working with reporters for a little while.

The murder house was different, though.

Because there was no renting or selling the Smith place, there was a lot of talk about tearing the house down and renovating the sizable acreage around it into something like an outlet mall. Red tape was the issue. The residence was far from the heart of civilization and accessed by a few very dodgy roads in need of re-paving—to say nothing of the trees to be felled.

Once the necessary changes were made, however, it would be a wholesome satellite of Monroe that would gradually fill in with apartments, suburbs, and other small businesses until it seemed to be one preplanned, unbroken town end to end. From one shopping mall—where Smith kidnapped his victims—to the other.

Where he killed those victims.

Jerry was overcome with a shudder as his car crawled to a stop before the rusted old gate.

There was a certain symmetry in it.

What would the victims have thought of these plans? He wasn't sure they would appreciate it, personally, but what did Jerry the real estate agent know about dead kids? He barely knew how to close. Pulling his coat tight against a bracing bluster of pre-dawn wind, still sharp despite imminent spring, Jerry fiddled with his key ring until he found the set he'd stolen from the office.

Whatever the victims would have felt about the site of their murders being plowed over with the parking of a place selling irregular Coach purses to drivers from the highway, he had a feeling they'd want one last shot at expressing their pain.

After all…it was one thing to read about the Smith house, or hear the case's details from your neighbor.

It was something very different to see the building in pictures or film.

And something altogether worse to see in person.

The facade brooded high above him, its every surface rotten and unkempt with the warping of years spent in neglect even before the Ripper's arrest. Averting his eyes from the eerie windows, the real estate agent told himself that $50 for unlocking a house was a sweet deal. He hurried up the creaking stairs of the front porch and unlocked the door, letting it swing wide to reveal the place before he stepped inside.

The day was a little cloudy. With no sunlight to shine in, Jerry dug through his pockets for his flashlight and let its high beam tell the tale.

Even with the light lending distinct shape to chairs and lamps and dusty end tables, Jerry somehow found the place looked black. His eyes read it all as black—as veiled in a fine miasma that drained everything of color.

Maybe it was just his imagination. Maybe he was letting his head run away with him.

Jerry had kids of his own, after all. His kids and Gary's went to the same private school, which was how he had first been subjected to the producer's forceful personality. And yet, despite having those kids, Gary had talked so casually on the phone about "the murder house piece." Like it was nothing. Like it was fiction.

Like eleven children hadn't died right there in that bleak, terrible house.

Trying not to think of how truly nightmarish it would be for anyone to spend their last waking day—hour, minute, second—in a place like the Smith house, Jerry swallowed hard and swept the flashlight beam along the wall. Upon finding a switch, he hurried to it and flicked it back and forth.

Damn. And he'd called the electric company beforehand! The real estate agency had been paying the bill more or less automatically while they debated whether to put money into renovation or demolition.

The problem was probably internal to the house, then...a fuse. God forbid, some wire in some wall somewhere.

Annoyed now, having ridden in this rodeo a few too many times, Jerry cast the beam of the flashlight around the dusty room, coughed a few times, and made his way in a promising direction. Kitchens were usually a good place to start.

Sure enough, Jerry found a door to the basement arranged around the corner from the sink. Sighing, he peered into the darkness that overwhelmed stairs tested by his flashlight's beam.

Something moved on the edge of the light and pulled itself out of sight.

Alarmed, Jerry leapt back to brandish the beam in the direction of the movement.

"Hello?"

The flashlight caught nothing, of course. All the same, he clutched his chest through his shirt. His heart pounded so fast it almost hurt.

Jerry closed his eyes.

Damn rats. Damn murder house. Damn Gary. Forget $50...Jerry was going to meet that son of a bitch at the door and tell him it was $150 or no deal. Between the risks to his career and his cardiac health, his time was increasing in value.

The fuse box in the cluttered basement seemed to be missing a fuse altogether.

This would be a problem for that idiot and his camera crew.

Groaning, the real estate agent rubbed his hand over his forehead and marched right back up the stairs.

The kitchen was cramped and disorderly, probably due in no small part to teens breaking in to mess around. How they got through (more likely over) the gate, now that was the question. Hammer & Croft really needed to get it together.

Shaking his head and sorting through drawers, Jerry said to himself, "No wonder I can't close a sale these days...who wants to even hear about these leads?"

At last, he located a pen and very old pad of paper whose leaves were ringed with cheerful illustrations of milk, sugar, and eggs. With the flashlight held in his mouth, Jerry scribbled a note for the television crew.

Somewhere in the house, something slammed.

His heart bracing itself against his ribs, Jerry stopped writing and looked around. His ears strained through the silence in pursuit of the faintest noise.

"Gary? That you?"

Nothing but his own voice echoed through the empty property.

Lips pursed, Jerry finished his note, tore it from

the pad, and set it on the spot of the kitchen counter that seemed the most obvious.

Satisfied, he dusted off his hands. Jerry made his way back through the empty living room, past the sheet-covered furniture and between a few abandoned cardboard boxes.

The very floorboards fell silent beneath his feet.

The Easter Ripper came screaming around the corner of the front hallway.

No—that was Jerry's scream.

It rose high and desperate, warbling with the knowledge of death even before the empty-eyed rabbit drew back its sickle.

Jerry gagged, astonished as his own blood splattered across the matted pink fur of the demon's bulbous head.

As his intestines slid out, Jerry reflexively caught them, cradling them back against his body as though they were an infant child. Thrown off balance by the unspeakable agony as his organs, heavier than he would have thought and felt as though liable to tug out his spine, he careened down to his knees and marveled that he didn't feel the slice itself.

It was everything else that he felt before he lost consciousness.

The burning sting and pulling cramp of the exposed viscera. Pulsing fresh blood and working flesh in his hands. The gaping open of his stomach wound.

The paw of the rabbit that bent to turn him over.

3

ON THE WAY to the Smith house, it was hard for Emma to say if the problem was the roads so much as the Channel 9 van itself. The roads were terrible, of course—literally dirt in some places, full of divots and potholes—but the van was so old and so small that she hadn't been surprised to learn its shock absorption qualities were entirely shot. It certainly needed new tires...and maybe a seatbelt or two.

From all the bouncing around everybody was doing, Emma's head hurt enough—but the constant bickering was giving her some second thoughts about whether the long-term benefits of interning for Channel 9 was worth the pain.

Tom slowed the van as they approached the open gate of the residence and Dana leaned forward, her nose wrinkled. She patted her beehive back into shape from its many brushes with the ceiling while emitting what was just another in a string of complaints.

"Eww! *This* place? I can't believe I went from the news desk to this!"

"You're lucky you *have* this job after the incident with the poodle," said Gary, barely looking over his shoulder from where he slouched in the passenger's seat.

"That could have happened to anyone."

But, to her credit, Dana gave up. She flicked an almost sheepish glance toward Emma.

While leaning back in her seat with her arms folded, the reporter asked the intern, "How's your ankle?"

Emma fixed the cuff of her sock to better hide the athletic bandage beneath.

"It's okay," she lied, "thanks for asking."

In sprinting down the hall to wrangle the poodle, Emma had rolled her ankle enough that it had very nearly broken. It was not as non-functional as that, but she was definitely more deliberate in her steps. She carefully tried it as Tom parked the car, rotating the joint left and right and finding herself satisfied that it could take a little bit of stress without much issue.

Gary tossed his cigarette out the window.

"All right, let's get started. We don't have all day. Where the hell is the real estate agent?"

As everybody got out of the van, the producer's beady eyes scanned the property through aviator sunglasses he even wore indoors.

"I agreed to give him fifty whole bucks to let us shoot this story...there's his car..."

An ugly old Datsun sat along a row of trees, far

across the wide lawn of dead grass. While Emma made her way up to the rickety porch of the dilapidated home, Gary muttered to himself again, "Where the hell is he?"

"The door is locked," Emma said, glancing back over her shoulder as she rattled the doorknob. Dusting off her hands and crossing back down the peeling porch, she told her boss, "Wherever he is, I don't think he's ready for us yet."

"Christ...intern—what's your name again?"

"Emma," she answered crisply, trying not to take too much offense.

"Yeah," said Gary, as if he had been testing her rather than ignoring her humanity for the past several months, "yeah, Emma. Make yourself useful and find us a way in, will you?"

"You mean, like—break in?" With a nervous glance over her shoulder, Emma said, "Don't you think we should just wait here for a minute?"

"I do *not* want to stand out here all day," Dana groused, arms folding around herself with a shiver. "It's fifty freaking degrees out here and I didn't bring my coat because I *thought* we would be going inside, *Gary*."

While the reporter shot daggers into the back of her producer's balding skull, said producer elegantly ignored her. Before Emma knew what had happened, Gary had slipped one ham hock arm around her slim shoulders.

He guided her toward the side of the house in an over-familiar way that she absolutely hated, saying, "Now, Emma, it's not breaking and *entering*! It's not even *breaking*, as long as you don't have to break a window...but, hey! If you find a window that's already broken"—he winked at her in a cartoonish way—"far be it from me to complain about you using it to get in!

"You just be an angel and get us inside. Let me worry about the ethics...we already have permission from the real estate agent. We're not going to be in any kind of trouble, I promise."

"But—"

"Don't take too long," said Gary, slapping her on the back of the shoulder before returning to the rest of the crew.

As their conversation resumed, Emma raked a grim eye across the property. Weeds had completely overwhelmed every square inch not already host to brooding trees or patches of withered leaves arranged in a pattern suspiciously resembling poison ivy. Emma grimaced, grateful that days spent bird hunting with her grandfather had taught her to avoid it and many other evil plants.

Maybe she'd find a side door unlocked. Everything would work out smoothly.

No such luck, of course.

There were no side doors. Only a rotting gray facade she followed through the high weeds while scanning hither and thither for snakes.

The wind picked up and whipped hairs from her bob across her eyes. A few locks stuck between her cheek and the big round frames of her glasses. Frowning, she removed them to polish as she walked a few more yards.

If there was a snake, maybe it was better to just not see it.

As she slid the frames back on her nose, Emma rounded the corner of the house.

Her vision resolved from the faded mess of unaugmented reality with a gasp.

It certainly wasn't that it was picture-perfect; and she would have had to press up against its dirty windows to confirm that every single plant was dead, so it wasn't that, either.

The greenhouse was just somehow so unexpected, and—frightening.

What was it about the little building? Who could possibly be frightened of a greenhouse?

Emma admonished herself for her silly reaction—but, all the same, the primitive part of her mind that once kept watch for lions in the savannah tried to find the source of the fear.

Then, it came to her.

The grayish panes of dirty glass; the dense vibrations of death emanating from within.

That little greenhousereminded Emma of a mausoleum.

That was it, exactly—a little tomb.

Shuddering, Emma turned her back to the hateful thing and reminded herself she was at work.

A back door mocked her with a window to the kitchen but an unyielding knob.

After jiggling it a few times, she pressed against the dusty glass with her hands cupping either side of her face.

"Hello? Real estate agent? Sir?"

Just where was this guy that he couldn't hear them, anyway? The house was big, but it wasn't that big.

Maybe he was up in the attic.

The attic, or...

Eureka.

A basement window was not only unlocked, but free to be pushed all the way into the house. The thing was small, but between the window well and the wide swing of the hinges, Emma was able to slide into the basement feet-first.

Of course, the landing was the hard part.

Emma hissed sharply as her bad ankle caught half her weight, her good ankle unable to take it all for fear of crippling itself in the process. Seeing stars after her brief explosion of bright pain, Emma stabilized herself against the brick wall and struggled to see through the darkness.

Not that there was much *to* be seen. After her eyes adjusted enough to define a few vague shapes, Emma used a mop and a stool to prop open the frosted window and permit a greater influx of light. Even with the overcast weather, this proved far more helpful than standing around in the dark. Grayish haze cut through the inky oppression and defined shapes like a washer, a laundry line, a fuse box. A switch on the wall, too. She tried it and frowned, looking up at the ceiling.

"This seems like it's the realtor's problem," she told herself with a shake of her head before carefully making her way up the dusty stairs.

And *what* dust! The place had been abandoned for all of three years, but Emma supposed three years was a very long time for a house to go without any cleaning. Add to that the fact that the last people in this place were probably cops bustling around to collect evidence, and, well…Emma probably shouldn't have been too surprised by the mess.

At the top of the increasingly dark stairs, she was stopped by a door against which she gently rested her hands.

Unlocked, thankfully.

What would she have done if it wasn't?

Shuddering, Emma banished the thought and let herself into the kitchen.

"Hello? Real estate agent?"

Nothing answered Emma but her own voice. More clutter everywhere; so hard to see past it was almost difficult to notice the doorway that seemed it would let her out toward the front of the house. Slipping through it, Emma made her way to the living room and breathed a sigh of relief. The front door stood just past another, down a little hall.

As she hurried through the living room, her foot nudged something that rolled.

With only a few seconds of hesitation, Emma stooped to pick it up.

A flashlight! Thank God...her eyes were really starting to strain. Smiling at it, too overjoyed to deeply question its presence, Emma straightened up and tried the beam.

Light poured across the eerie room of stored furniture, each piece draped in white sheets. As though the souls of the davenport or the footstool were bound to the house more tangibly than any murder victim.

It was strange to think about a murderer as being a person who lived in a house. A real human being with a mother and father—maybe even a brother or sister. How were *they* traumatized by what their relative had done? How did it affect a person to discover that someone they knew and interacted with on a regular basis was a sadist with blood on their hands?

Emma shivered. God willing, she would never have to know the answer to that question. If someone she cared about turned out to be a killer like the Easter

Ripper, Emma wasn't sure she would be able to keep her own sanity.

Frankly, she wasn't sure she was going to keep it now.

The beam trained on the floor before her, Emma navigated the haunting living room while keeping a close eye out for loose nails or anything else that might have damaged her already tender foot.

She was so focused on looking for objects *on* the floor that Emma didn't notice the floor itself until she had almost exited into the front hallway.

Then she stopped.

Slowly, Emma glanced back the way she'd come. She let the flashlight beam do the seeing.

In a house full of dust, the living room floor was clean.

4

THE PAIN WOKE Jerry up.

It was amazing he could awaken at all.

Amazing, and horrible.

An instinctive cry pierced his lips at the hateful pain of his disemboweled innards tugging parts of his torso he couldn't identify. Some muscle, some *thing*—ah!

He couldn't think about it. Jerry couldn't even bear to think about it, oh God. His eyes closed and his coppery mouth opened as he tried to breathe.

Breathing, of course, only agitated him more.

It made him think of his organs moving around on top of him instead of inside him.

His organs, exposed to air.

God, God!

Jerry tried to open his eyes to see where he was. 'Tried,' because they twitched naturally toward the slimy pile of viscera that had been dumped atop his wound. Part of an intestine looked like it had been squished flat, and—was that dust? Oh, God, were his organs *dirty?*

He had to suppose he was lucky it was all still attached. Yes, yes. Somehow, some way, his organs were still attached to him. If he could just keep (What was *that*? His spleen? Oh, Christ, he shouldn't try to guess!) his organs kind of close to the wound and figure out a way to call for help, the paramedics or some genius surgeon would be able to tuck it all back—

Bloody bile and whatever was left of his morning donuts raced up his esophagus and burst out of his mouth. Jerry sobbed to spit up on himself like an overgrown baby and groaned in agony at the subsequent pain.

How? How had all this happened?

Jerry was so focused on the pain and the horror of his current condition that he couldn't even remember how he had gotten this way. He shut his eyes and thought about his wife doing her weird Eastern breathing exercise whenever her aerobics got strenuous. He had no idea what she was doing—it involved a lot of huffing and puffing, sort of like childbirth, so it was probably some sort of woman thing—but he had a feeling that trying to control his breathing was a good idea.

He hissed air out through his gnashing teeth, then slowly blew it through his rounded lips like he was blowing through a straw. The breaths he allowed back in were only the smallest and most necessary ones.

He could afford to move his chest and torso only so much, and filling his lungs to any useful extent made him feel like the wound was tearing open and more was falling out.

Soon he was trembling a little, but at the very least he was no longer groaning and kicking and thrashing about on the hard surface of...wherever he was.

Where was he, where was he?

Oh—no.

The murder house.

Jerry had come to open the murder house. He had come to open the murder house for that fat, greedy producer, and he had gone to the basement and come back up, and he had written a note, and—

And then—

Tears rolled down Jerry's cheeks, squeezing past eyes that remained scrunched shut because he couldn't stand to even accidentally look at his organs. Even thinking about them was too much. The wet red-gray-pink viscera recalled the towering rabbit being splattered in his blood.

The Easter Ripper.

This was impossible. The Easter Ripper had been executed the year before. Was this some sort of bad dream? A psychotic break?

Yeah. Yeah! Maybe that was it. Maybe this was a, what-do-you-call-it, a "delusion." A fantasy. Jerry wasn't as hip to psychiatrist stuff as the Mrs. was, but he was smart enough to know something that was too insane to be real.

And this?

Him in this cold place, organs hanging out, arms wet with blood, throat and mouth burning with tangy bile?

Disemboweled, maybe even killed, by the Easter Ripper?

That just couldn't happen.

That couldn't be real.

Jerry couldn't be *murdered*. Murdering was for other people. Jerry was a real estate man. He wasn't a soldier or a criminal. He was a guy in his forties who still nursed dreams of running his own agency and getting a chance to manage other salesmen for once. He had so much to live for! He had so much to do.

And his kids. What about his kids?

Jerry couldn't die. Not here. He realized now that death could always get him at any time, and that there was nothing he could do to stop it from swooping in.

It had always been there—waiting.

But today couldn't be that day. It couldn't.

This was all some wild dream influenced by his call with Gary. Jerry would wake up soon.

Any minute.

And you know what he'd do?

He'd kiss his wife's sleeping head and say, "Sorry I haven't been home enough lately, baby."

And then he would pick up the bedside phone.

He would dial Gary's number.

And he'd say, "Take your fifty dollars and choke on 'em, you slimy, tracksuit-wearing imitation Dumbo, the deal's off."

Jerry nodded against whatever surface he'd been lain upon in this dream-world of his. His eyes still closed to avoid seeing the hateful contents of the nightmare into which he'd stumbled, Jerry tried to discern where he lay without having to look.

Someplace cold and hard.

Linoleum?

No, not quite.

A door opened somewhere: all part of the dream.

This couldn't be a linoleum floor. It was curved somehow. His neck hurt, propped forward by whatever he was lying on. Through the fever of his pain, his dreaming mind sought the answer.

Someone lay a hand upon his head.

His wife, waking him up.

"I know," Jerry cried, his eyes flying open, "a bathtub!"

The rusted sickle snagged the flesh of his throat and tore in, the cruel curve of the blade slitting a bright red valley across his windpipe.

Jerry's eyes and tongue bugged from his head as a great fan of blood spritzed across the cold face of his killer.

Their eyes met for what seemed to be an eternity—until the blood reduced from a violent pump to a lazy drizzle that echoed the laconic pull of death upon Jerry's mind.

The killer turned away for a few seconds, then turned back to Jerry with something in his grip.

He opened one of Jerry's limp, red hands.

Through careful manipulation this fiend slid a cold object into Jerry's palm, closed the dying man's fingers around it and lowered the attached arm to let it rest upon his bloody chest.

The realtor struggled to watch through the haze of blurring eyes as the killer patted his cheek and departed, but his long vision was failing. Unable to see anything but what was closest to him—a common effect in dreams, at least in Jerry's—Jerry looked down at himself at last.

At least he couldn't see the organs anymore. They

didn't even bother him. Not only had they become the least of his problems—they didn't even hurt anymore. Was this shock? Death? Was there a difference?

Jerry lifted the smooth, strangely shaped object in his hand. What was it? Not quite round. Delicate, but hard.

Almost like…

An Easter egg.

5

MAYBE IT WAS silly to be so disturbed by a detail like an out-of-place clean floor.

At once, Emma concocted all number of plausible explanations. For instance, maybe this was what the realtor was busy doing somewhere in the house. Maybe he was tidying up here and there for the shoot.

Granted, that begged the question of why he would do such a thing to begin with. Why would you clean a floor, for instance, without moving some of these cardboard boxes out of the way? Why wouldn't you dust a little?

Why would you care at all about cleaning any part of a miserable murder house, even if it was about to be shown on a news special?

Emma wrapped her arms around herself, suddenly feeling more off-kilter than before. The flashlight tucked in her elbow, she studied the front hall.

Dust everywhere again...except for the parts where there were footprints, and one fairly long, wide streak—as though a piece of furniture or a rug had been dragged along the hall, around the banister of the stairs and up to the second floor.

"Hey, intern! Emma! You in there yet?"

Emma stirred herself from her reverie at the shout from the front lawn. She was obviously just unnerved by the environment. When everything from an innocuous greenhouse to a not sufficiently dusty floor was scaring her, it was a clear sign she needed to grow up.

After placing a hand over her forehead, Emma strode to the hall's termination and opened the front door for the rest of the crew.

"The real estate agent's not answering, assuming he's still somewhere around here."

"Well, maybe his car broke down and he had to walk back to town...whatever. Saves me fifty bucks. Come on, people, let's scout our location."

Once Gary barged past Emma, Dana clacked in and regarded the dim foyer with a sour expression.

"Smells...musty."

"Smells like perfection," corrected Gary, spreading his hands to demonstrate the residence around. "Look at this place! It's exactly what we need. Creepy, crappy, and very dramatic."

Emma smiled politely as Tom passed her, because it was safer than responding to Gary's comment about the place by saying; "Guess you and this house have a lot in common, then."

Instead, she turned and lifted her eyebrows in attentive expectation as Gary said, "Chop chop, it's time to hustle. Grab all the equipment from the van and get it in here. We're going to get set up."

No point in getting annoyed. This was her job, after all.

Her unpaid, unappreciated job.

But Emma had to admit...she was really starting to look forward to the day that she could tell Gary where to shove it.

"I can do that," she said as he turned away, "but there's a problem."

"Oh, boy. What is it now?"

"Well—the power's out."

"Then turn it back on!"

Emma scoffed helplessly toward the other two people in the room. In her early twenties, as she was, Emma was always saddled with the vague sense that other adults were somehow "more adult" than her. They were therefore privy to a wider array of practical knowledges and solutions than she was. Tom and Dana, however, looked at each other and then at her, both of them totally useless.

"I don't know how," she settled on telling him, shaking her head and spreading her hands.

The response was the most infuriating thing of all. With a wave of his hand, Gary turned away, patted his pockets for a new cigar, and told her, "Then figure something out," while walking down the dark hall and around the corner to the living room.

In the hopes of getting his help, Emma glanced one more time at Tom.

"This is sure one amazing house," he said unhelpfully.

Biting back a sigh, Emma quite literally rolled up her black-and-white-striped sleeves and made her way back to the basement.

Don't get her wrong, the house was still incredibly creepy—but Emma couldn't help thinking the flashlight was a divine gift. If a rat or a spider were about to attack her, at the very least, she would see it. She swept the beam across the tiles of the kitchen floor and along its walls, locating the same back door through which she had previously strained to see.

After hurrying over to unlock it, the beam alighted on a strange door that had no knob.

She frowned, decided trying to see within was futile, and turned back around to head to the basement.

The flashlight illuminated a note sitting on the kitchen counter.

Hurrying over, Emma glanced only briefly at the kitschy stationary before squinting to read the text.

Gary—

Looks like someone broke the lock on the basement window and got in the house since the last time I was over here. They stole the goddamn fuse, so the power is out. There's another fuse around here somewhere but I don't know where. Left the front door open for you in case I don't hear you drive up, so if you read this note and I haven't heard you yet, just shout.

—Jerry

Emma frowned, reading the note one more time to be sure. She had definitely shouted for the real estate agent—more than once, both inside and outside the house. Was this some kind of weird prank? Maybe he really was up in the attic.

Or deep in the depths of the basement, where the flashlight revealed the monolith of a black doorway had been waiting for her discovery the whole time.

She listened, hovering back at the bottom of the stairs while calling toward that ominous room, "Hello? Jerry?"

Nothing.

Biting her lip, Emma edged into the basement.

It disturbed her to think that open doorway, yawning into a hateful abyss of black nothing, had been there while she was oblivious in the darkness. Anything could have come out to frighten her.

Anything, or anyone.

Palms sweating, Emma raked her flashlight around the basement's laundry room and sighed to notice a workbench against the far brick wall. Upon hurrying over, Emma studied its contents with a frown of uncertainty.

The pathetic truth was that she didn't really know what a fuse looked like. What kind of jerk broke into a houseto steal a fuse, anyway? What purpose would that serve? Maybe that Jerry guy was making stuff up to cover his ass. Maybe the power really had been off the first time he came, and he just forgot to—

Emma's blood froze in her veins.

Her heart pounded in her ears as she yanked the note from her back pocket.

The flashlight held in her mouth, Emma smoothed the note upon the workbench and read its text one more time, now paying full attention.

Left the front door open for you

"He left the door open?"

A leaden weight where her stomach used to be made her lean forward against the workbench.

If the real estate agent had left the door open—then somebody had to have locked it. It *was* locked, right? They had tried it from the outside. Emma had, anyway.

Was she wrong? Had she wasted all that time? Hand on her forehead, Emma deliriously walked herself back through the events of the past few minutes and tried to decide if she was losing her mind. She really *did* unlock that front door, didn't she?

But then...

Who locked it after Jerry opened the house?

Lips tight with anxiety, Emma glanced aside and tried to think what all this meant.

Among dust even thicker than the stuff that coated all the objects upstairs, Emma's eye caught a little round object that triggered long-lost memories of watching her father change a fuse.

Breathing a sigh of relief, Emma focused on getting the lights turned on for now. That would reduce her anxiety better than standing in the dark basement, rationalizing away her fears that someone had broken into the house and was there with them that very minute.

It was all ridiculous, of course. She made her way over to the fuse box while chiding herself.

Who on Earth would have the least bit of interest in breaking into a house like this? There were no valuables to be had; that much was obvious from the exterior. Nobody but the real estate agent knew they would be there, so it wasn't some crazed person trying to get on television. And if teenagers happened to be in there to graffiti the place and were hidden somewhere in the house, Emma had to figure they'd sneak out when the coast was clear.

Either way, it seemed like it just wasn't her problem.

After discovering a little clip on the flashlight that allowed her to attach it to her shirt rather than hold it between her teeth when she needed to use both hands, Emma opened the fuse box, found what looked like a spot where one was missing, and screwed the replacement in after blowing it free of dust. Then, with a little prayer under her breath, she hit a likely switch.

Something thundered so angrily behind Emma that she screamed and whipped around, woefully unprepared to fight anyone or anything.

The washer rattled in a way that seemed to indicate it, too, was ill equipped for confrontation.

Emma's shoulders sagged with relief. She laughed a little, although that laughter was tense.

Just what was rattling around in there? Clanging and banging like any minute the glass in the door was going to shatter? Emma's lips pressed into a thin line.

She sort of had the feeling that she really didn't want to know, but she tried the door just to say she had.

Stuck, thankfully.

Nodding to herself, Emma turned to head back upstairs.

The pale child darting up the stairwell, the back of his yellow shirt just caught in the beam of the flashlight, made her scream again.

6

JUSTIN LEAPT UP in the photo booth. He felt panicked; as though his mother were jostling him awake an hour past his alarm, telling him in a frantic voice that he'd be late for school.

That was where he should have been. Where was he, instead? It was so dark here—where was his nightlight?

Oh.

Oh no.

Justin sat up a little straighter to remember what had happened earlier. Oh, no, oh, no! With a quick hand, he drew the curtain wide.

Monroe Mall was empty, dark, and silent as the grave.

Justin's palms broke into a sweat immediately, his heart pounding like a frightened deer's. His eyes, accustomed to sorting out the shapes of his bedroom in the darkness, struggled to make sense of the vast ceilings and broad floors of the shopping center.

Where was his mother? Had she given up the search for him and gone home to wait? Surely she hadn't decided to leave him there to punish him. And it wasn't because she didn't care, right?

Right?

Justin's stomach twisted, his young mind concocting all number of insane and terrifying ideas. No—he was being ridiculous. Of course, his mother loved him. She wouldn't just leave him because he was a coward.

Because he was afraid of an Easter Bunny.

Now that he'd had some sleep and awoken to find himself in a far more urgent situation, Justin felt like a real doofus. How had he been so afraid of the Easter Bunny that he had run *away*? So what, the costume was stinky. A whole bunch of people probably had to wear it, so it stank. And his weird breathing? Justin realized now that he'd probably breathe pretty weird too if he were in a get-up like that.

But, it was just—

Those eyes.

Those staring, staring eyes.

Black as the mall around him.

Arms folding around himself, Justin called, "Hello?"

His voice bounced satisfyingly through the vaulted halls of the shopping center, his own cry echoing him back in a mimicked greeting devoid of meaning or comfort.

"Mom?"

Another empty bounce lowered to a resonant hum that soon thereafter faded into nothing.

"Can anybody help me?"

Apparently not, confirmed the echo.

Justin looked in anxious suspicion around the mall. It was a little hard to figure out what he was supposed to do above all the wild things his mind presented him with.

For instance, bogeymen aside, his father had once told him that department stores used to let vicious dogs loose on all the floors to keep burglars at bay during the night. Was that true? Did they still do that? Did they do it in malls? Where would the dogs be now, *if* there were dogs?

Boy, maybe Justin really was a scaredy cat.

He tried not to be, but as he thought more about the dogs—and about the snippets of that scary zombie movie set in a shopping mall, gleaned while peeking through the staircase banisters as his parents watched it in the living room—he became more and more pressed by his urgent need to find a way out.

Maybe some boys would think it was fun to be trapped in a mall. It did occur to Justin that he might try to make it fun, but he quickly discovered that anything of interest—all the restaurants in the food court and stores on all floors—were locked with big gates, like cages. Justin shook one, his omnipresent frown deepening as the gate showed no signs of giving in to his slight strength...whatever it amounted to.

But things only got worse from there.

After deciding to go back the way he'd come, Justin marveled. The dark mall seemed so much bigger without anyone else in it. It made him feel even smaller than he did when adults were around.

He had never wanted his parents so much in his life.

Especially as he at last lay eyes on the empty gazebo

where the Easter Bunny had been taking pictures.

A chill swept over Justin, his neck dimpling with fear in response to the sight.

It was wrong. It was wrong to be in a mall after closing. Malls were meant to be busy, crazy, full of light and color and people. This mall was just dark and empty.

And, at its heart, this empty chair set within the spiraling web of ropes which had once guided the labyrinthine line.

Without the rabbit, the chair somehow resembled an open mouth emitting a long, steady scream. Anguish perpetually rising while the little boy looked on in horror.

Folding his arms around himself, Justin hurried past the holiday station with his gaze averted. He plunged on into the dark, his vision having adjusted enough to leave him confident there were no dogs.

No, no dogs.

Only another, far greater gate, this one stretching floor-to-ceiling in the hallway and cutting him off from any possibility of reaching the front doors.

Tears filled Justin's eyes, frustration raising in his heart. Now what was he supposed to do? Just stay there all night, he guessed. All the payphones were up by the front doors, too. And could he even use them when the power was off for the night? That was the sort of question he could have asked his father.

Now Justin had no one to ask.

Justin was all alone in a terrible, empty mall with no place to go and no option left but to look for a staff member.

Maybe there weren't dogs, but there had to be somebody, somewhere. Security guards? Maybe even just a janitor?

It didn't matter who it was. As long as they were an adult, they could help Justin get home.

His eyes reddened by tears, Justin did a lap around the mall's other side and gradually trailed back to the food court.

In that zombie movie, there had been a very scary part where things happened in the back parts of the mall. The staff parts. That was the only reason Justin understood those places existed. He kept an eye out amid all the caged stores and soon, gasping in relief, he found it in an innocuous corner near the food court bathrooms.

A door! A door, not out, but deeper into the mall—to regions not meant for customer eyes.

Fingers crossed, Justin rushed forward and tried the knob to find it unlocked. With a cry of amazement, he rushed into the well-lit white tunnel of the staff hallway beyond.

And right away he was confronted face-to-face by a bleak "missing persons" poster.

HAVE YOU SEEN THESE YOUNG GIRLS?

The bold typeface caught his eye; the pictures gave him the same numb feeling of scary speculation inspired by the faces on milk cartons.

The details terrified him.

Both of these children disappeared on a trip to the Monroe Mall. They have been missing since April 14th, 1982. If you have any information concerning their disappearance, please contact the Monroe Police Department.

Justin looked at their faces, their names, their ages. 10 and 11 years old. And another missing poster—he saw it when he turned around. The boy on it?

The boy on it was 8 years old, just like Justin was.

He also went missing at Monroe Mall.

And he had gone missing that very same year: 1985.

Just a few weeks before.

Suddenly breathless, Justin devoted himself to finding help immediately.

His steps quick, he made his way down the long white hall and tried to peer to the end. So far as he could tell there was one door at the end, a number of others scattered along the way, and what looked like one hallway off this one.

At that juncture, Justin paused to see where it led.

The swinging door at the end was labelled 'STAFF RESTROOM.' He leaned in, calling, "Hello?"

His voice echoed through the big, eerie bathroom that reminded him of the one at the movie theatre. Seemingly endless stalls lined both sides and vanished around the corner, the only space not taken up by toilets taken up instead by sinks and big mirrors reflecting Justin's animal desperation right back at him. Tugging at the collar of his t-shirt, he turned around and tried the hallway again.

There had to be offices somewhere, and offices would have either people or a working phone—maybe even one where he didn't have to pay. Figuring the doors at the far end of the hall were his best bet, Justin made his way to them.

He was no more than twenty feet away when the door at the end of the hall burst open.

A sharp scythe covered in dry blood held high

above its head, the Easter Bunny rushed out toward Justin.

A scream tore from the boy's lungs, mingling with that awful, rising wailing from before that seemed to come from nowhere and everywhere in his panic.

Justin whipped around and sprinted forward, trying to block out the terrible groans of hunger that seemed to emanate from the creature. Maybe it was his imagination. Maybe it was too many zombie movies. But the bunny was here, it was definitely here—and it was coming to hurt him now that his mother couldn't help.

Unable to imagine any other options, Justin dashed back into the staff bathroom, picked a stall at random, and shut himself inside with his hands over his mouth and his body crouched back against the cold surface of the toilet.

The thought of filth never crossed his mind. Justin's every instinct was focused on nothing but survival.

As the door to the bathroom slammed open, those instincts told Justin to stay very, very still.

Beneath the stall, Justin stared through the dark and soon caught a flash of pink amid the shadows. The rabbit advanced down the row of stalls, its steps slow and deliberate.

It paused two stalls before Justin.

The stall door banged open with a noise like a gunshot.

Justin flinched but did not substantially move, his eyes squeezing shut and his breath freezing in his lungs.

The rabbit's steps moved on, each slow and steady footfall echoing cruelly through the bathroom. They charted the course of his path down the row of stalls, past Justin's, and on to the next. This one, right beside Justin's, the rabbit arbitrarily slammed open in hopes of surprising prey.

One single stall away from death.

Justin flinched again, but did not move or cry out.

After another contemplative pause, the bunny resumed its slow, steady steps. Now they carried it around the corner, and when the third stall slammed open, it was far enough away that Justin was not rattled by it.

Now, he simply listened and waited.

Soon enough, another door opened; this, on the other side of the bathroom.

The footsteps ended altogether then.

Justin released his breath as that same distant door swung shut.

There was another exit. That was good. Justin let himself out of the stall, deciding to go the opposite way as the Easter Bunny and out the way he came. He'd find a nice faux palm tree in the food court to fall asleep under, huddled where the rabbit couldn't find him. Then, first thing in the morning, he'd call his parents and have them pick him up.

He wouldn't tell them anything about the Easter Bunny, because they would assure him he was dreaming, or making it up, or imagining things.

But he was not imagining things. The Easter Bunny was evil.

It was smart, too.

For instance, it had somehow managed to lock the bathroom door through which it had followed Justin.

Panic surging through him, Justin searched for a lock on his side and failed. He rattled the handle a little before, worried about making noise, he bit back a sob and leaned against the frame.

Now what was he going to do?

What he was going to do before, he guessed...find an adult, or an office with a phone. Only now he had to do it while avoiding the Easter Bunny.

Luckily, by the time he got up his guts enough to open the other bathroom door and peek into the hallway, the rabbit was nowhere to be seen.

Justin realized he was trembling only when he stepped into the white brick hallway and gingerly eased the door shut behind him. At the last second it slipped from his small fingertips and slammed, leaving him wincing in frustration and terror. Should he go back and hide?

But—no. After waiting for a few seconds, Justin grew satisfied that the rabbit had not heard him.

His fingertips numb, his head ringing with panic, Justin made his way down the length of the hall on somewhat unsteady legs.

More missing children posters littered the corridor. Many children had been disappearing from Monroe, and for as many as six years.

All of them disappearing around Easter.

Especially from the mall.

Justin made it past the vending machines with a lingering glance of desire. Was it wrong for him to steal from such a thing (if he could) while trapped all night? Maybe his parents could pay the mall back the next day. He was just thinking about trying to reach into the dispensing slot.

Then—he heard it.

The creaking open of a door.

Pale, Justin pressed himself to the wall like he'd seen spies do in movies. His heart drowning out almost all other noises, Justin scooted to the end of the hallway and slowly peeked around the corner.

The shriveled old janitor almost smacked his mop into Justin's shins like they were playing ice hockey.

"Oh, excuse me! Say—"

"JANITOR - JACK," as his nametag read, lowered the headphones of his Walkman and let it hang around his neck.

"What the heck are you doing here, kid?"

"You've got to help me!"

Lunging for Janitor Jack and clinging to his arm, as though this stranger were his own father, Justin gazed up through a veil of stinging tears.

"The Easter Bunny's trying to kill me," he explained in an urgent whisper.

Janitor Jack frowned in a quizzical way.

"Whoa, calm down."

Leaning his mop against the wall, Jack bent down and took the boy by the shoulders. Justin's tears spilled over at once. His mother had held him that way while they were in line. While she was trying to convince him to sit with the Easter Bunny.

"Now, how'd you get back here?"

"I—I was here with my Mom, and she wanted me to—take a picture—"

The boy fought back a few sniffles and, patiently, the man said, "Uh-huh."

"And—and the Easter Bunny was staring at me, and I didn't want to do it—and when I did, I got scared and I ran, and I fell asleep, and—and it doesn't matter! The Easter Bunny has gone crazy!"

Janitor Jack's brow knit deeply enough that all the wrinkles in his face doubled in depth.

"Easter Bunny," he said under his breath.

"I'm not making it up! He's been chasing me! We have to call the police."

"Hold on."

Guiding Justin to the nearby office door, Janitor Jack punched in a code. His fingers moved too quickly for Justin to follow, but it didn't matter. The janitor led the boy in and said, "You wait here. I'll go check it out. Don't worry—you'll be locked in."

"But—"

But, nothing. His headphones blasting a creepy song about there being something wrong with the moon, Janitor Jack pulled the door shut before Justin could protest much more. Stomach flipping with anxiety, Justin looked around the back office he had searched for all night long.

Was there a phone? Was there a weapon? Was there anything that could help him? That old man meant well, but the Easter Bunny would have no trouble using that mean-looking scythe of his. The old janitor wouldn't stand a chance.

Would it be Justin's fault if the guy died?

The boy's tears ran anew while he hurried through a break room and into a small set of assistants' desks.

And on each desk, a telephone.

Hands trembling, Justin rushed to the nearest one and yanked it from the base. Quick as he could, he did what he had been taught to do in an emergency situation and dialed '911.'

But from the first tap of the first button, the phone made a protesting noise.

"Night mode engaged," the device told him. "To dial out, please deactivate night mode."

All the blood drained form Justin's face.

One time, he had gone to the office with his father.

At the end of the day all the employees had been forced to do something similar. That way, at night, the calls to the office would be routed to some other service; a switchboard that basically just existed to tell people when the office would open again.

Was there some way to reach the switchboard? Was there something helpful written on the phone? Justin hung up the handset and took the cradle of the device in his hands, turning it over and looking for any slip of paper, any post-it note—anything at all that might have instructions on how to dial out at night.

And then the lights died.

Justin cried out and dropped the phone. As the handset swung away from the base the boy scurried to the manager's office back behind the secretary pool. Scrambling in there, Justin rushed to the one place he could hide: the desk.

Throat tight, the boy leaned against it in an effort to see out the window that overlooked the assistants.

Justin spread two slats of the blinds and peeked through the window as subtly as he could.

The same darkness that had drowned the mall now swallowed all its back offices. Palms sweating, the boy struggled to make out any form.

He hoped for a ringing telephone triggered by some automated process on power failure.

Maybe even Janitor Jack or the cops, coming to tell him that he would be all right. That everything would be all right, and he could go home with his family again.

Instead, the door to the staff offices creaked slowly open. The footsteps it announced arrived with a pair of tall ears.

Muffling another fearful cry, Justin shut the blinds and slipped beneath the desk as quietly as he could. Trying his best to keep his trembling under control, Justin drew his knees to his chest and sat under the desk with his arms wrapped around his shins. There, quietly rocking back and forth, Justin listened to the footsteps.

Closer, closer.

The steel of the scythe ground out against something, singing cruelly in the air.

Tears ran down the boy's cheeks as the footsteps stood on the threshold of the room.

Justin braced himself for the appearance of the same feet he had seen on the other side of the bathroom stall.

Any second, he was going to die.

He had to accept that now.

Any second, the Easter Bunny was going to run in, swing the scythe and cut his guts open.

He'd be another missing child plastered all over these back walls.

Maybe somebody else, some other kid, would see him right before they met their end.

As all these thoughts flashed through his head, Justin waited for the rabbit to enter the room.

When the Bunny's black eyes and buck teeth bent down beneath the desk, Justin realized he'd entered it already.

7

EMMA STUMBLED BACK against the wall, one hand on her heart and the other barely able to hold the trembling flashlight.

Was she seeing things now?

After her wave of fear-induced paralysis passed, Emma flipped on the basement light at the nearby switch and looked up the stairs.

That had been a kid, hadn't it? A kid in a yellow shirt and blue shorts, with a black mullet.

Where had she seen that kid before?

Then again, if there really had been a kid, well— it seemed impossible that her colleagues upstairs would have missed him. He was running pretty fast. If any of them were in the kitchen, the living room, or the foyer, they would have seen him go by. And if he went straight out the back door, well—even Emma, down in the basement, would have heard it bang by now.

In other words…if there really were a kid, she probably would have been aware of her colleagues' reactions.

Upstairs, nobody seemed to have noticed anything. Emma kept her trap shut other than to cough as she walked into a big cloud of Gary's acrid cigar smoke. She waved her hand before her face, grimacing to turn on a kitchen light.

"The hell was that scream about— Say, the lights are back! You got the equipment in here yet?"

Emma coughed again as she banished the cloud. "No, but—"

"Well, what are you waiting for? Come on, kid, time is money! Shut that light off, though—I don't want another fuse problem."

She obeyed reflexively, insisting, "But that's just it!"

Glancing toward the doorway as Tom appeared to listen in, Emma told him and Gary both, "I don't think we're alone here."

Tom frowned, his arms folding over his loose-fitting Hawaiian shirt. "What do you mean?"

"I mean I just saw a kid."

"A kid? Where?"

"Running up the stairs. You didn't see him?"

Gary laughed. "Sweetheart, if I saw a kid runnin' up these stairs, I'd have offered him your internship position for standin' around! Now come on!"

The producer's free hand drew back to wind up for a totally unwelcome, one hundred percent uninvited, incredibly creepy swat of the seat of her shorts.

Time seemed to slow down.

Emma's instincts, finely tuned to detect and avoid

creeps, orchestrated a spring forward enough inches that his meaty hand missed her and instead swung lamely by his side.

In conversation, at least, Gary didn't miss a beat, ignoring her anger-reddening face as he said, "Let's get this show on the road and get back to the studio! I got a complaint to level with Hamster & Craft, or whatever it's called…"

With a resentful roll of her eyes, Emma let Gary lumber down the stairs before shaking her head at Tom.

She didn't like to go into her feelings with coworkers, but she couldn't help it.

"What a creep! Sorry, I've tried to keep it to myself, but…Gary's a real jerk sometimes."

Tom shook his head, his hands sliding into his pockets with his sigh. "You're not kidding. *I'm* sorry you have to deal with him. Have you found any sign of that real estate agent?"

"Nothing yet."

"I wonder where he's at…well, let me know when you have my camera out."

Emma repressed a noise of annoyance as Tom wandered off into the house.

What a clueless jerk! A little help would have been nice. Even just the offer.

Out on the lawn, Emma studied the contents of the van and the many black cases within. Dana stood near it, smoking a cigarette that she put out as Emma dragged the first black case out into the open.

"This story is a load of bull," said Dana, apparently deciding they were friends now that Emma had twisted an ankle on her behalf. "What are we even doing here? You should see my script! It's total trash."

"Well, I mean, it is sort of a puff piece."

"'Sort of!'" Dana laughed harshly, glanced into the truck as though considering lending a hand, then decided against it with a quick thought of her manicured nails. Her arms pumping at her side as she hurried after Emma to talk the burdened intern's ear off, the reporter lowered her voice to say, "You're damn right this is a puff piece. It's worth nothing! There's not a new piece of information in it. There's got to be a *real* story somewhere in this house...so many locked doors."

"I swore I saw a kid running up the basement stairs just now," Emma said, eliciting a roll of Dana's eyes.

"Oh *please*, Emma! I thought you were way more down-to-earth than that. *Ghost* stuff? That's the kind of nonsense I'd expect Gary to come up with. He's probably planning to have you wear a sheet and run through the background of a shot or something...just keep your eyes peeled, okay?"

Looking conspiratorially around before stepping into the house and leaving Emma to haul the equipment by herself, Dana said, "Locked doors upstairs...the one missing a knob in the kitchen...I mean, come on. I don't think anything around here is what it seems."

That was for sure. The knobless door had bothered Emma and still did. What was up with that? Was the Easter Ripper really some kind of sick, game-playing mastermind?

Had he really only killed eleven children?

'Only.' It seemed like such a disgraceful word to use when you were talking about the deaths of children. The tortures and murders of children.

Even so, anybody who knew anything about the

Easter Ripper had the distinct sense he had more victims than were attributed to him.

That boy in the yellow shirt—was he a victim of the Ripper?

No wonder Emma had the sense she'd seen the boy before. He was probably one of those kids whose picture was plastered all over the news in the months surrounding the arrest and trial of Anthony Smith. It was an ugly, unavoidable story, and it wouldn't have surprised Emma to discover she had unconsciously absorbed the features of the kids' faces. In fact, that notion helped her rationalize why it was probably just a figment of her imagination rather than something like a ghost.

Dana was right. Who could believe in ghosts, after all!

After almost ten minutes of hauling, arranging, dragging and sweating, Emma had managed to get everything into the house; another ten, and the lights were set up.

"All right," said Tom, tweaking his camera's settings a bit more before looking up at Dana with a placid smile. "I'm ready if you're ready."

"*Absolutely*. Let's get this over with."

"Ah, don't act so crucified." Waving his hand from where he perched upon a nearby packing crate, Gary dug a handkerchief from his pocket and used it to daub his forehead. "You're getting a free pizza lunch. Not too shabby to be fed on top of your usual paycheck."

"Don't patronize me, Gary," said Dana, adopting her even-keeled reporter voice. "I swear to you, one of these days I'm going to take this microphone and shove it right up your—"

"Can you move to the left?" Tom waved her over,

glancing into the eyepiece of his camera while Emma picked up the boom mic. "That's better, thanks."

"Anyway, Gary"—Dana switched to her normal voice and smiled in a manner intended to be charming—"I was thinking we could—"

"I don't pay you to think, Dana. I pay you to read the goddamn script."

"I hate this job."

"Well, pull it together!" Puffing on his cigar as he shoved his handkerchief away, Gary nodded to Tom. "We good to go?"

"Yep. Lighting's great, camera's rolling."

"All right. Ready? Action!"

Like a trained robot or a dog whose job was to salivate at the sound of a scientist's grant-purchased bell, Dana became a different person.

All trace of her sardonic personality fell away. At once, she was a proper reporter: Channel 9's best and brightest, for whatever that was worth. Her cool tone slid professionally up into the boom mic Emma held suspended above her head from off-camera.

"Anthony Smith, more commonly known as the Easter Ripper."

Dana recited her script with ease, her memory sharp as a tack. Between that and her talent for reporting, Emma had to admit a certain admiration for the woman.

It was just her attitude that was the problem.

"The mere mention of his name sends shivers up the spine of parents across the country, his horrible murder having left lives shattered—and families, ripped apart."

With a look of dramatic intensity on her face, Dana slowly strode toward the camera while declaring,

"Tonight, we'll go inside the now-vacant home where eleven innocent children spent their final moments in agonizing pain and terror.

"Untouched since those horrible crimes, some say his spirit still haunts the home till this day. I'm Dana Turner, and this is a News 9 Special Report. Silenced Tears: Inside the Home of Serial Killer Anthony Smith."

"Cut!"

Gary waved his cigar, puffed it, nodded sagely and said, "Yeah, that was good. Real good. Let's take a break."

"Gary, I think I want to redo the line where—"

"This isn't 60 Minutes, Dana. It's not even Channel 5. We're not here to win a Pulitzer."

Her face contorting into a scowl, Dana said, "Fine. I'm going to find a place in this gross house to fix my makeup."

"And I'm going to take a leak," announced Tom less delicately. "So you're going to have to look someplace other than the upstairs bathroom you were planning to hog."

Rolling her eyes in annoyance, Dana stormed toward the front hall. Emma glanced at the boom mic in her hands and lowered it upon a nearby cardboard box, watching as everyone else around her dispersed.

It was strange to be behind the scenes of something like Channel 9 and learn how little work was really involved in putting together a story like this one. The truth was that Dana would end up actually working for about three or four hours on the whole report. She might do an interview or two, a little narration, and film whatever bumper scenes they filmed there on-location. When it came to footage, Tom would get all the eerie background shots of the property that would play below her voiceover.

The hardest part about being a reporter, it would seem, was working with people like Gary.

Alone again, Emma was consumed by a shudder. She thought about poking around upstairs to see if the realtor was around, but the idea of running into another phantom kid freaked her out too much...and, frankly, if he hadn't shown up by now, Gary was right. The agent probably had ended up needing to hitch a ride back to town for some reason.

Instead of worrying about yet another problem, Emma followed Dana while thinking of their brief, almost friendly conversation earlier. Where had she gone—upstairs? Not outside, surely.

The only other option then was...ugh.

A squat little door poised under the stairs.

Emma's aunt and uncle had recently sold a house with a little door like that...another murder house, coincidentally, but that was another story. Such doors made her skin crawl, but at least to this one's credit it was a little larger than the one that notoriously creeped out her cousin. Rather than the door for, say, a tucked-away boiler or storage crawlspace, this one seemed more like a cupboard.

Emma knocked lightly upon it and waited, her guess soon paying off.

"Gary?"

"It's Emma."

"Oh, thank God. Come on in...if you can find room."

No kidding. The little cupboard was cramped... and creepy. The under-stairs space was illuminated by a bare bulb in the ceiling: poised directly beneath it, Dana used a cracked mirror glued to the wall to reapply her red lipstick. Bedding had been arranged on the floor, and a pillow seemed to indicate it was once a makeshift resting place for somebody...or some kind of a prison.

"I don't think I even want to know," said Emma, more to herself than to Dana.

The journalist laughed and capped her lipstick, dropping it back in her purse before coming up with a compact of powder.

"You won't get far in this industry with that attitude, but I know what you mean...doesn't this place just give you the willies? I swear"—she raised the puff and rapidly tapped her nose with flesh-toned powder—"as soon as we're back at the station, I'm writing a letter to Channel 5 to see if they have any job openings...I heard Christa Freemont is going on maternity leave soon, and I can't imagine she'll be back. The producers over there are better than Gary, but not by much."

"Isn't there somebody you could complain to?"

With a wry but somehow sympathetic look—as if she at once pitied and envied what she perceived to be some naivete *lot* in Emma—Dana clapped shut her compact and dropped it in her purse. With her newly freed hand, she patted Emma's.

"The sad truth, honey, is that in this industry—and probably a lot of others—women who complain don't last very long. You don't have to stand there and take it...but you should also be careful about protesting too loudly."

While Emma suppressed a grimace at this painfully old-fashioned and oppressive piece of so-called advice, Dana smiled elegantly and returned to the mirror. Fixing her beehive, she said without looking,

"Would you be a dear and fetch me a drink of water? I am *parched*."

'Fetch!'

Luckily for Emma, it was easy enough to turn a set of gritted teeth into something resembling a smile... but even when they'd had a bonding moment, Dana had a way of really grating on her nerves.

Emma knew the older woman meant well, but the reality was that Dana had made herself part of the problem at Channel 9. No wonder there had been so little competition to intern there...anybody connected enough to the networks to even get an interview at Channel 5 probably knew that Gary and his producer buddies were creeps to be avoided.

Speak of the Devil—Gary rooted around in the cabinets of the kitchen where Emma had only intended to get Dana that cup of water. Emma managed a courteous nod, then went right to looking for a cup.

This was a little more difficult than anticipated. A nest of spiders had moved into a portion of the counter where a few disgraced dishes still sat, never to be cleaned. Emma did not immediately see a cup in their midst, but she had to confess a certain degree of clutter blindness afflicted her. The counters were covered in odds and ends, ranging from appliances that were meant to be there to the contents of emptied drawers—not to mention items that were taken from other rooms or moved during the course of the investigation.

And, as Emma struggled to parse the scattered odds and ends, Gary's watery eyes remained fixed on her from behind their sepia lenses.

She only discovered this when she glanced his

way, about to make casual conversation to break up the uncomfortable feeling of being in a room with somebody so silent.

Whatever she was going to say, she forgot it beneath the skin-crawling stare.

Gary fixed the collar of his pink shirt while saying, "You've been doing a good job today, kid."

"Emma," she told him, "and thanks."

Her eyes flickered from him and, more urgently, across the sink. She studied flowerpots and mixing bowls, then at last found a somewhat rusty tin cup that had to be some kind of antique. Wrinkling her nose at it but finding nothing better, she switched on the water and tried not to grimace as the pipes groaned their protests. Taking advantage of the delay due to such a long period of disuse, Gary sidled closer.

She willed the water to hurry.

"I saw you using that boom mic back there," he told her, chucking her in the arm with his fist and ignoring the way she winced.

An evil brown sludge splattered out of the faucet, like the house had hocked a loogie. As a slightly less disgusting, but still decidedly brown, water came flowing out after, Emma gritted her teeth. Come on, come on. Get a little clearer, already!

Her boss never missed a beat, his great form looming closer all the time. "You were like a pro with that thing...seems to me you're a natural in this industry. I didn't know what to expect when you showed up, but you're proving more valuable all the time."

No time to waste. She settled for tan as an acceptable color of water and filled the cup.

"Great," she said, "thanks."

Emma shut off the water, grimacing at how hard the knob was to turn. She looked down to rectify her grip on it, adding additional pressure with her palm, and at last the valve closed.

And while she drew her hand away, she noticed the strange piece of metal lying along the back of the sink.

The crowbar was nearly flush with the corner of the counter and the wall; she might never have noticed it if she hadn't been busy looking anywhere but Gary.

"Play your cards right, and this could be a big opportunity for you." The greasy idiot went on, breathing thirstily down her neck. "If you see what I'm saying."

"Uh-huh," said Emma, mostly to herself.

She had tuned Gary out almost completely—tuned the nonsense of her job out completely—and lifted the crowbar from where it discreetly lay. While she raised it and turned it around in her hand, Gary made a little noise like a nervous laugh. He stepped away so fast that by the time she turned around he was already halfway across the kitchen.

"I'll be sure to keep that in mind," she told him automatically, forgetting the contents of what ought to have been grounds for a sexual harassment suit.

While the producer's eyes whipped from Emma to the crowbar in her hand, Emma thrust the cup in his direction and said, "Could you bring this to Dana for me? I have to go do something really quick."

"Oh," her boss said, so taken aback to be given a request by the intern that he didn't know how to respond as Emma pushed the cup into his hands. "Oh, uh, well—"

"Be right back," she said, hustling down to the

basement that had once been terrifying but was now the subject of serious interest.

This was what Dana was talking about—the "real" story. What was in that washer? Was there some invaluable piece of evidence that the police, oblivious to its existence, had left untouched since the crimes?

Worse—yet, for Channel 9, maybe better—was it some kind of murder trophy thumping around in there? A hand?

A head?

The idea was awful but somehow exhilarating. If Emma discovered a thing like that, maybe the station would finally give her a paid position!

Downstairs, Emma inspected the rattling washer and tried its locked door. For whatever reason, the cycle seemed to be stuck. They had been there easily an hour or more, yet the washer showed no signs of stopping.

This crowbar was the only way. She might have kissed it, if it weren't so rusty.

Breath held, Emma slipped the prongs of the crowbar into the door of the washer. She had never had occasion to use such a thing before, but it was easy enough to figure it out. A little bit of leverage, applied by leaning into the prier, produced a promising groan from the old machine.

A few more pounds of pressure and the washer produced an alarm as the door burst open.

Emma jumped back, the crowbar slipping free from her hands without the door to provide resistance. As the washer's rotation came to a stop, the intern took a deep breath and bent to inspect the contents of the machine.

A doorknob?

Frowning, Emma removed the round brass object and turned it over in her hands.

Yes...this was definitely a doorknob. But—

It dawned on her after only a second.

Emma gasped, springing from the cold basement floor and letting the crowbar remain where it fell.

With the knob clutched like a precious treasure, Emma rushed back up the basement stairs and through the now empty kitchen.

The knobless door received its missing piece with promising ease.

For just a second, Emma considered calling her coworkers to let them experience the discovery with her.

But, well...did they really deserve to?

Emma did everything they wanted at the drop of a hat. Even Tom took advantage of her from time to time, or at least failed to do the decent thing and offer to help her when he had a spare moment. The whole day they had been at the Smith house, Emma had done all the grunt work without a single complaint.

Committed to enjoying the first moments of this discovery by herself, Emma turned the knob and let the door swing wide.

On the other side, the dead bodies of her colleagues floated in a pool of blood.

8

DANA'S BLANK EYES stared forever at the ceiling; Gary lay face-down in a collection of his own viscera; Tom was supine on the ground, a bullet wound blooming from his chest.

The entire room screamed red as though the walls had been coated in blood, and the screaming rose up inside Emma until a hand dropped upon her shoulder.

"Emma!"

Dana's voice—unexpected, inexplicable—snapped Emma out of her vision.

The bodies disappeared.

Shocked, Emma whipped around to find Dana and Gary standing behind her, their looks varying from concerned to annoyed.

"But," babbled Emma, "but I saw—"

"What?" Eyes whipping nervously around the newly accessible parlor, Dana asked, "You didn't see a rat, did you? I hate everything about this."

"N—no." Sweat dotted her brow and, wiping it away with the back of one trembling hand, Emma took in Gary and Dana through her sea of endorphins.

They were all right.

They were all right!

But would they still be all right when this shoot was through?

"Where's Tom?" Looking frantically between the two of them, then back over her shoulder into the empty parlor, Emma said, "We should find Tom."

"Somebody's getting a little bit of an attitude today! 'Bring Dana this water,' 'We should find Tom.'" Poking her in the shoulder with one fat finger, Gary said in a snide way, "*You* should find Tom, little lady, and while you're at it move the lights in here." Gesturing around with that still pointed finger, Gary said with a glance over the rims of his shades, "Seems like a great room to shoot in."

Emma's teeth clenched so tight she felt they might shatter in her skull. She wanted to scream about what she had seen—wanted to say out loud the words, "I think I've had a premonition—we should all go home."

But would they believe her? And if she did convince them to go home, what would come of it?

Emma would lose her internship. That was what would happen.

Fired from Channel 9? Forget it.

She'd never work in journalism again—not in Monroe, anyway.

"I'll get started moving the lights," said Emma with

a sigh, hoping Tom would wander back before she had to go look for him.

While Gary nodded and strode off in satisfaction, Dana called after him, "When are we going to eat, Gary? You promised a pizza lunch in exchange for this torture."

"For God's sakes, will you people quit making these unreasonable demands of me? If *I* can wait, *you* can wait. Let's shoot one more segment before we start thinking about that."

Glowering, Dana turned to Emma once the producer was gone. "Try and make it snappy, okay? I'm *starving*—and besides, I want to get out of this creepy place as soon as possible."

Without another word, Dana ditched the intern who was left fuming in the doorway.

What a bunch of jerks! They had barely even noticed the parlor. Not even acknowledged that she had stumbled across it. Rest assured, when stories were being told about the segment—if any—Gary would take credit for the discovery.

And this discovery might be worth talking about, Emma found.

Now more dedicated than ever to taking her sweet time moving the lights, Emma wandered into the stuffy old parlor.

It was dark within. There were windows, yes, but they were shuttered—and the shutters, boarded shut from inside the room.

Folding her arms around herself, Emma meandered farther in and raked her gaze across the uncovered pieces of furniture that had absorbed, in addition to a layer of dust, the clearly increasing attacks of some resident family of moths. The antique red armchair was worn and collecting holes in the corner of one upholstered arm. The empty fireplace's mantle was coated in a layer of dust so thick that Emma wasn't sure the room had been in use even before Anthony Smith's arrest.

But the photographs on the walls?

Emma had the definite feeling that they had always been this way—since maybe even before the murders.

The walls, the mantles, even the end tables: every horizontal surface had at least one photograph. One at a time, Emma studied them in their dime store frames, her hand lifting to her mouth in quiet amazement.

This was Anthony Smith.

And not just Anthony.

This was Anthony Smith's *family*.

Emma had the eerie sensation that she was intruding somewhere truly private by looking at these things, but she couldn't stop herself. It was her job. And, anyway, didn't a murderer forfeit their right to privacy when they committed their crimes?

So, Emma looked. She looked, and she learned something that had not been reported widely in the press. That, to her knowledge, had not been reported at all.

She saw the family life of Anthony Smith—who was, in almost all pictures, depicted with another boy of his exact height, frame, and hair. They even had the same ears.

Were they twins?

Hard to say.

Every time the brother appeared in a photograph, his face had been torn through.

The same was true with the mother. This hollow-faced woman, a neck and torso and head of blonde hair along with an occasional hand, appeared in a great many photographs with smiling little Anthony.

He had been a cute kid. Dimples glowed in his cheeks, and his dark eyes had a life that was just not there at the time of his execution.

Maybe his brother had once possessed such a similarly happy air.

And then?

And then—then, Anthony Smith became the person he was always meant to be.

Then, the Easter Ripper took shape.

With as little as was known about the Ripper's family life—about this brother that Anthony apparently had—Emma was willing to bet good money that this brother was Anthony's first victim.

This seemed especially likely because there were no photographs after the boys were about twelve, but that didn't mean anything. Teenagers got strange about cameras and family events. People got lazy about getting pictures developed.

Still…it all struck Emma as very strange. The haunting pictures, this family with holes for faces.

And, brightly smiling, Anthony in every single one.

Her skin crawled.

Emma averted her eyes and turned to get the lighting equipment.

The Easter basket sitting on the table caught her eye.

Lips pursed, Emma slowly approached the basket. Was it possible for it to still be booby-trapped after all this time?

But the nearer she drew, the less likely that seemed. She edged closer, frowning deeper, bending to inspect it where it sat upon the secretary beside the door to the room.

Much like the living room floor, the basket bore not a trace of dust.

No.

No, no.

That was it.

Emma had had it.

There was something going on.

Glancing sharply around, Emma backed out of the parlor and hovered on the edge of the kitchen.

What was going on? Was this all some prank by the realtor?

Maybe they were trying to make the house seem somehow haunted so as to—what? Perform tax write-off voodoo for an unsellable murder house? Advertise it to macabrely-minded potential buyers who might see the segment? Commit some kind of *Scooby-Doo*-esque insurance fraud?

It was all too weird. The knob in the washer, the clean parts of the floor, the basket.

The visions.

Frankly, Emma hoped this really was some silly *Scooby-Doo* nonsense. The alternative was that something was *really* wrong here. The alternative was that this house was being haunted.

Haunted, or—

"I don't hear equipment being set up!"

Nostrils flaring, hands clenching into fists at her sides, Emma glanced in the direction of Gary's voice and grudgingly moved to obey his command.

But all the while, her mind worked.

Was this opportunity at Channel 9 *really* that important to her?

Look at the facts. In exchange for exactly zero dollars an hour, Emma had twisted her ankle, done all the grunt work, come to a murder house, and was now potentially endangering herself at the behest of Channel 9. She had worked for three months, and half her colleagues barely knew her name. Day by day she became increasingly aware that the environment in which she toiled was not just oppressive, but exploitative and misogynistic.

And yet, she was still there.

Why?

Because it was a good opportunity.

That was what she kept saying to herself. That was what Gary kept saying to her.

But was the opportunity really that good when you got right down to it? Would that many doors be opened by working for free at a station with the poorest reputation in Monroe? Was interning *anywhere* and giving her labor away at no cost really going to help her earn the respect of someone like Dana? Like Tom?

Speaking of Tom...Emma was starting to worry about him. Where was he? Still upstairs somewhere? By the time she had finished with the lights she had convinced herself she had no choice but to check— and that checking for Tom would be one of her last duties at Channel 9.

She just needed to quit. Plain and simple. The decision swept over her in a moment of perfect clarity as she set up the final light, turned it on, and stepped back to inspect the arrangement of the set.

Yes: this would be her last day interning for Channel 9.

If they didn't like it, she'd leave it off her resume. It was probably better unmentioned anyway. She'd get a good job doing something else—maybe something like answering phones at the newspaper. Answering phones *for a paycheck*, mind. When the Monroe Star had reaped the benefits of her service for a year or two, she would take her experience and apply for a real position at Channel 5.

And then...

"All right, looks like we're ready to go." Clapping his hands as he strode into the parlor, Gary looked around in approval while Dana trailed behind. "Let's do this."

"But what about Tom?" Emma gestured toward the living room and the stairs beyond, saying, "I was just about to—"

"Forget it. If we wait any longer, Dana's going to go on strike."

"Oh, please, Gary. Like *you* aren't just as excited for the pizzas as I am...probably more."

"Just get over there, wise guy...you, intern girl, work the camera until Tom gets back."

Oddly excited for the opportunity even after having come to the conclusion that she needed a change of pace, Emma said, "Are you sure?"

"Ah, it's nothing. You were great with that boom mic, and the camera is even easier. A monkey could do it...it's why we hire guys like Tom." Laughing cruelly, Gary picked up the cumbersome device from where it sat on the nearby armchair. He dumped it into Emma's hands, saying, "Don't sweat it, kid. Just point and shoot."

A bit of shuffling later and they were rearranged, with Gary holding the boom mic and Emma uncertainly training the camera on Dana.

"The rampage started in late March 1979, when Smith walked into a local mall and took a seasonal position as an Easter Bunny. A job meant to spread joy and cheer put him in the perfect position to abduct young children until his capture and execution in 1985. Many of the bodies have not been recovered.

"As told by survivor Randy Martinez, Smith would release the children in his greenhouse and force them to go on a deadly Easter egg hunt while he stalked and murdered them. Three years later, many say he still haunts the home he grew up in."

Still in her serious reporter tone, Dana slunk toward the camera while earnestly saying, "Is Anthony Smith, executed in the electric chair, back from the dead? Back for revenge on anyone who enters his house? We may never know if I starve to death before I get the pizza lunch promised to me by my worthless producer."

"Dammit, Dana!" Incensed, Gary nearly dropped the boom mic on her head—or smashed it on the ground in a fit of rage he barely managed to overcome. "We nearly had it."

"I *want my lunch*," Dana said, swinging the microphone down against her skirt and staring daggers at Gary. "I can't work under these conditions! There are farm animals treated better than this."

"Fine! Let's take a break. Hey, intern girl, go take the van and pick up some pizzas."

Setting the boom mic down more delicately than he had been about to before, Gary fished his wallet out of his back pocket and presented Emma with the golden company credit card, along with the keys to the van.

"And grab me a sub, too. And a container of wings."

"*I* want wings," said Dana in the tone of a jealous child.

"Too bad," said Gary, "I distinctly told you 'pizza.' Wings are a privilege, not a right."

While Dana and Gary continued grousing, Emma looked down at the card with a barely repressed sigh.

"All right," she said, turning away, "I'll be back soon."

"'Soon!' Make it pronto."

Almost biting off her tongue at Gary's ridiculous correction, Emma focused on what a satisfying experience it would be to quit at the end of the day while she made her way through the empty rooms of the Smith house. Twilight had begun to paint the sky outside a dusky red and the light bled into the house to make it seem the world was on fire.

Maybe, in a way, it was.

Emma stepped onto the porch and saw it right away, but for some reason her brain just couldn't interpret what it was looking at.

Frowning, shading her eyes with her hand, Emma tried to make sense of the Channel 9 van still parked on the other side of the Smith lawn.

As though it were a wild animal, Emma made a slow approach. By the time she arrived, she felt like she was going to throw up.

The Channel 9 News Van had been dismantled. Its tires had been removed, its hood had been popped to reveal the destroyed engine within, and a note had been stuck to the passenger's side window.

From somewhere in the house, Dana screamed.

9

EMMA WASN'T THE only person in the world with big dreams. You think Dana Turner didn't once believe she would go down in the history books as one of the world's great reporters? Of course she did.

She used to believe a lot of things. That people were basically decent. That they were professional.

Gary disabused her of both those notions, proving over the years that he was willing to do anything for a buck. There was no story he wouldn't swipe out from under a hardworking journalist, and there was no depth to which he would not sink in an effort to cover it up.

This was why Dana was putting so much faith in the intern's ability to snoop around the house and find a good story. Gary barely knew the girl existed and therefore wouldn't think twice about any investigating she was doing; if he saw Dana so much as look at a picture too closely, in seconds he would be hovering over her shoulder. Asking her opinion, deciding to incorporate it into the piece, telling her what words to say about it...

All this was to say that Dana just hated Gary. She hated his nonexistent ethics and hated being alone with him, as she was when the intern left the house.

"I don't know about you," said Dana to Gary, squinting at him through his omnipresent cloud of cigar smoke, "but I'm starting to worry that Tom fell into whatever trapdoor we'll find Jerry in."

"Oh yeah! That damn real estate agent." Turning the cigar around in the corner of his mouth, Gary puffed on it and stared off into space. "That is some weird stuff. Doesn't seem like him to miss out on 50 bucks."

"Or leave his car behind. I'm telling you this place is *creepy*, Gary."

"Which is what makes it perfect for the story! Look, there's all of three more segments to get through. Just slog through 'em and I promise, when the station sees how well the piece does, we can have you back on the desk by Christmas."

"By—"

Dana stopped short and shut her eyes, willing herself to stay calm. "Well, if you think you can do it, I would appreciate you getting me back there."

"Sure thing, baby. You know I'd do anything for you."

Pinching her cheek as though she were a child, the ape waddled toward the kitchen and left Dana scowling in the formerly sealed parlor.

Great! Now her make-up was smeared again.

Shaking her head and reflexively patting her beehive to keep it in shape as she did, Dana picked her way across the dusty floor of the creepy old house.

What an awful place. Even if a bunch of kids hadn't died here, it would still be creepy. Its windows were all too big, its bookshelves emptied by looting or family, its floorboards were creaking and often broken. Everything just seemed hollow and wrong, like the little cupboard with the mirror where Dana intended to fix her make-up.

She tried to, anyway.

When she tugged at the half-sized door, it was stuck.

Frowning, Dana tried the knob with a little more vigor.

Now that was funny. It had turned no problem earlier. Had it locked when she left to answer Gary's nasty water delivery? She hadn't thought there *was* a lock.

Dana tried the knob again, tugging on the door as she did.

It almost budged—almost, for a fragment of time that amounted to less than a second.

Then, it didn't.

It reminded Dana of being a kid, when her brother would hold shut the door to his room after kidnapping her favorite dolls.

Somebody was holding this little door shut.

Dana scowled, banging on the frame.

"Tom! What are you doing in there?"

No response. She rattled the knob again to find it unyielding. At last, she gave up, falling back upon her heel and slapping her own thigh in frustration.

"I can't believe you. You're such a weird dude. Are

you *hiding* in there? Come on, we've got a shoot to get through! Wait, let me guess—you'll be out of there just in time for the pizza, right?"

Still nothing.

Dana rolled her eyes and crossed her arms, bending toward the door to scornfully say, "I know you're in there. Is this supposed to be some sort of joke? It's not funny. It's just annoying. The intern had to hold the camera—who knows what kind of shot she got! She probably cut my freaking head off."

When there was still no answer, Dana dropped her fists to her sides with a glower a person could see through wood.

"Fine, jerk. Be that way. See you when lunch is here."

Although Dana stormed toward the stairs as though to find an upstairs bathroom and fix her makeup there, she hesitated by the banister.

Dana slipped quietly out of her patent leather heels and forced herself to stand on the dirty floor in her stockings.

So, Tom wanted to mess with her?

Well, she could mess with him right back.

On the balls of her feet, Dana crept back to the strange little door. It was only about as tall as she was, and with most doors at least two feet taller it produced an unnerving effect.

Not as unnerving as throwing open the door to reveal the gigantic, bloodstained rabbit on the other side.

Dana screamed higher than she'd ever screamed before and leapt back in surprise.

Half a second and she thought it was a joke.

Half a second more and the rabbit raised its sickle.

The rusted blade swiped through the air and sliced up the left side of Dana's face, its jagged blade hooking up into her eye and bursting the sac of ocular matter as though it were an egg full of new spiders.

Dana screamed again. The world went red with blood and death-adrenaline and the fire alarm bells of absolute panic.

Her face hurt. What a scar she would have someday! Oh God, how horrible, oh—she would never be on television again.

At least, not the way she had wanted to be.

The rabbit lowered its huge head and burst through the door, its black eyes and mockingly dead affect as intent on Dana as was the next swing of the sickle.

Motivated into motion by the intentions of this second blow, Dana screamed through the pain and scrambled off toward her right. She stumbled forward, tripped, landed momentarily upon her hands and knees, then sprang back up before the rabbit had even had time to turn.

The rabbit?

No.

The Ripper.

That was the Easter Ripper.

Sobbing, unable to fully comprehend the state of the injury that made her kick her own shoes and smash into the banister because she was now half-blind, Dana rushed up the stairs and used the rail to pull herself faster than her feet could fly alone.

Behind her, the rabbit advanced step by deliberate step. It did not rush, but instead walked with its sickle high. It moved this way as though to say its catching her was inevitable, and that it did not want to waste energy before it did.

"Help," screamed Dana, launching herself onto the second floor and looking desperately around, "help, Tom! Gary! Emma!"

Dana rushed blindly down the hall, no more able to see where she was going than she was aware of what her options were. She hadn't been up here for more than five or six minutes total. What were the rooms like? For all she knew *all* the doors up here were locked—at least a few, as Dana herself had said to Emma, certainly were.

With her right hand on the wall, Dana dashed along and used her remaining eye to peer through the veil of blood surging from her forehead down her brow. Choking on her tongue between sobs, she used the knob of every door she felt.

Two were locked. The third was not. She had no idea where she was and didn't care. Feeling around once again, she sought anything that might hide her.

A generous wardrobe of some kind offered her safe harbor for a moment. She had a good feeling she could fit and did, sliding in and pulling the door shut behind her.

Hyperventilating in the dark, Dana struggled through the pain and panic to think more than urgent, animal thoughts.

The problem was twofold now.

Were there other places to hide on the second floor of this hellish place? If not, she would be easy to find.

But the quantity of hiding places may not have mattered...because the more pressing issue, and the one that occurred to her as the Ripper stepped into the doorway of the room, was the awful question:

Had she been leaving a blood trail?

Panting for air as she was, Dana settled on holding

her breath to preserve the sanctity of her hiding place.

But it didn't matter.

Nothing mattered anymore.

The room was silent

Dana's lungs burned.

Her eye watered.

Blood and ocular matter slid down her face and stained her suit, which had cost two hundred bucks.

She was going to die.

She was going to die.

She would never buy another suit. Never wear another piece of clothing.

The Ripper threw open the door, having moved as silently across the room as Dana had when sneaking up on that evil little door.

Before she could even shout in surprise, its sickle slashed through the air and severed her arm at the shoulder joint.

The 'thump' as Dana's arm fell to the floor seemed even louder than her cry of agony.

10

EMMA STARED AT the dismantled van, her heart pounding, the urgency of the situation rising.

What was happening in there?

What had happened out here?

Though she knew it was absolutely pointless other than to discourage her, Emma dashed into the driver's side and tried the key for rote. The engine did not even make an attempt to turn over, its key moving a pitiful twenty degrees and locking there to silence. Tears were already rolling down her face by the time she gave up, jerked the keys from the ignition and tossed them angrily at the smashed windshield.

She should have listened to her instincts. As soon as things seemed bad—as soon as she saw the out-of-place clean floor—she should have resigned and insisted they radio back for a taxi to get her home.

Instead she was here, panicking in the dismantled

news van while a scream rang out from within the murder house.

Remembering the premonition with a chill, Emma leapt back out of the useless van and intended to respond to the scream—but it was followed by another, even more horrible one that was so blood-curdling she paused.

And in that pause, she remembered the message.

Teeth clenched, Emma slowly neared the passenger side of the van and inspected the note displayed there. The handwriting was a struggle to parse, uneven and frantic—but too much so, somehow. Like someone pretending to be insane to avoid being pegged as a calculating monster.

> *NOWHERE TO GO NOW*
> *LOOKS LIKE WE'LL BE PLAYING A GAME*
> *YOU'LL BE HUNTING EGGS*
> *I'LL BE HUNTING YOU*
> *FIND THEM ALL AND YOU CAN LEAVE*
> *DON'T FIND THEM*
> *AND YOU CAN'T*

A cold scream rose in Emma's mind—not the scream of terror that had been produced from within the house just now, nor the scream she had uttered when seeing the awful premonition she ought to have heeded.

No. This long, rising scream was like a choir of voices, all the elements of her own soul coming together to orchestrate an alarm signaling absolute danger. It was her intuition lighting a fire that prioritized one thing and one thing only: survival.

After tossing the note aside, Emma rushed to the

shut gate and rattled it upon its hinges. She clenched her teeth while assessing the height and wondered if she could make it over—then wondered if she would be able to get back to town before whoever was doing this chased her down.

Who was doing this? What did it all mean?

Was it real?

"Help," screamed Dana from inside the house.

Pale with fear, Emma rushed back in through the front door and skidded to an immediate halt.

There was no doubt something truly awful had happened. This time, the vision didn't go away.

The trail of blood from the half-sized door to the top of the stairs was very real, and very static, and very clearly related to whatever had caused Dana to abandon her designer heels on the floor.

"Dana?"

Hoping Tom or Gary might come to the endangered woman's aid so that she wouldn't have to, Emma paused for a few seconds before another, altogether more horrible scream echoed from the second floor.

Something thumped somewhere.

Wincing, Emma made her unsteady way upstairs while doing her best to avoid the trail of blood.

She had just made it to the top when Dana, her blood pumping in great, splattering waves from the stump where her right arm used to connect to her torso, came sprinting around the corner.

"Help me," she screamed in as desperate a voice as Emma had ever heard, "help me! He's killing me!"

Emma froze, then backed toward the stairs in horror.

The Easter Ripper burst around the corner and, with one pink paw, grabbed Dana by her bloodstained, disarrayed beehive.

"No," screamed Dana, "no, no, no!"

The nasty sickle drew back only to arc forward.

Emma watched, her mouth open in horror, as the rusted blade hacked straight through the reporter's torso. While Dana Turner's lower half dropped limply to the floor along with a few organs and a large portion of her spine, the ripper hacked into her again. Now he caught the blade in her sternum and had to jerk it back out, a lung or maybe her heart punctured by the error spurting blood out across the hall.

At last, with one final stroke, the killer sliced completely through Dana's neck.

Whatever remained of her body fell to the floor, leaving only her gruesomely disfigured head, still oozing the ruins of her eye, in its extended bloody paw.

Screaming as she had never known she could, Emma fled straight down the stairs.

The image replayed itself endlessly: Dana's body, hacked to pieces right in front of her. Dana Turner, the real Dana Turner, a woman she had grown up watching on television and now personally knew—that person had just been killed. Right here, right now.

And if Emma didn't figure out something to save herself, she was going to be next.

By the time she was in the living room, her ankle was stinging with the exertion. She was going to need some kind of weapon.

With a reluctant look around, Emma limped into the kitchen and paused only to try the back door. Upon confirming it had been sealed somehow, Emma gritted her teeth and limped down the stairs to the basement.

It wasn't as dark as it had been before, but the idea of getting trapped in here didn't sit well with Emma. However, the basement was the only place she knew of that had a potential weapon. The rusted old crowbar still lay on the floor before the washer. She snatched it up and held it to her heart, even more grateful for it than she had been before.

Just what was going on here? There was no way this was a prank—and if it was a ghost, it was a solid one.

It was almost like the Easter Ripper was back, but that was impossible.

The Easter Ripper was dead.

Her hands tightening into fists around the crowbar, Emma decided that it must have been a copycat killer of some kind. They just had a very realistic costume and implement. That was all.

And that explained what happened to Jerry the Real Estate agent…probably Tom, too.

Emma's stomach sank to think of it.

This Jerry guy, Tom, and Dana—all dead.

Now—well, now all that was left was…Gary.

It was almost enough to make a girl want to wiggle out of the basement window and run away on foot.

Sighing, Emma looked down at the crowbar in her hands and assured herself that the decent and human thing—the *right* thing—was to help her boss, no matter what a scumbag he could be.

The problem was figuring out where he was.

Cautiously whispering the producer's name, Emma made her way into the unexplored rooms of the basement with her crowbar at the ready. Had Gary heard the commotion upstairs and known to hide? Had he made it through the back door before the Ripper—or Ripper-lookalike—locked them into the house?

Wherever he was, Gary wasn't in the basement. The old-fashioned cellar was unfinished concrete full of storage containers and old pieces of furniture. Each room was dirtier than the last. When she came to the final room, stopping short at the uncanny sight of a mannequin standing—armless, legless, lifeless—in the middle of the floor, her concerns about Gary were disrupted by the presence of a locked door.

Glancing over her shoulder, then edging toward the door, Emma examined it. Kind of heavy-looking, but it resembled an internal door rather than an external one. Was this to yet another room?

She tried the knob. Nothing—locked.

Frowning, Emma released it and turned around.

The Easter Ripper filled the doorway behind her.

11

THE BASEMENT ROOM in which Emma found herself cornered was not the largest in the house by any means, but it was better here than someplace like the kitchen. If she could just slip past him and make it upstairs!

Then?

Then...she'd figure it out.

For now, the Ripper made his deliberate way toward her, sickle raised high in the air.

"Stay back," Emma demanded, brandishing the crowbar before her, "don't touch me!"

The sickle slashed and Emma dodged aside, a series of cardboard boxes tottering over amid the sound of shattering china and a broken cuckoo clock getting in one last squawk. Crying out, Emma leapt away from the broken pieces and just barely upended the mannequin in time to take the next hack for her.

This second one had just missed her. She wasted no time sprinting toward the doorway of that dangerous back room—

And her right ankle exploded in a starburst of pain as she landed on it too hard.

Hissing, Emma stumbled forward and tried to regain her pace only to find herself reduced to a slower limp for now. She paused in pain and cursed—but when the rabbit's form loomed up behind her, she spun around to face it.

The Ripper extended one great pink paw to grab her as it had grabbed Dana.

"No!"

Her scream echoing through the basement, Emma drew back the crowbar and smashed it into the killer's arm. The rabbit stumbled back, disoriented, and Emma tore her gaze from the beast's black eyes to speed-limp for the basement stairs.

Too soon, the Ripper regained its footing and carried on after her.

At the top of the stairs, Emma burst into the kitchen and made a quick decision. There was no time to catch her breath or nurse her ankle. There was only the ever-pressing drive to escape: to go wherever she had to go to avoid being killed the way Dana had.

That awful crimson mist of blood made Emma's eyes water with its most recent appearance in her memory. The shock on Dana's face, the horror—the hefty *thud*s of her body's pieces falling to the floor, where they still lay in a pool of their own crimson fluids while Emma made her way upstairs.

She did not look.

She could not look.

Averting her eyes, Emma made an immediate right

and continued up the stairs to the house's attic. The door creaked so viciously that she winced, afraid the Ripper would be attracted by the noise.

"Gary?"

Emma's whisper was as low as it could be, but it still felt much too loud. With a suspicious glance over her shoulder before slipping in and shutting the door behind her, she took in the contents of the room and all its dusty charms.

This creep sure did love mannequins. Three more of the limbless dress forms were impaled on their stands, the three of them arranged in a little triangle as though permanently gossiping despite their headless state. Emma eyed them uneasily while on her way around the room, checking drawers and opening cabinets.

No sign of her boss...but something was amiss up here.

Emma wouldn't have noticed it without her flashlight; there was only one bulb in the whole attic.

With the beam before her, however, Emma noticed it yet again as she swept the room.

The dust.

Having noticed it the first time, it was all she noticed now. Someone had been moving around this house. They were transporting and moving objects—maybe bodies, among other things—to achieve whatever goal they had in mind.

In this case, that goal seemed to be the protection of a hidden passage.

The flashlight drew Emma's attention to a pair of long tracks that had been dragged into the heavy dust on the attic floor. Emma studied it, as well as a set of old footprints just barely distinguishable to her.

These seemed destined for the same cabinet that was adjacent to the scrape marks on the floor.

Crowbar tucked under her arm, Emma threw her slight weight against the cabinet's side and dug her heels into the floorboards.

The cabinet creaked in protest, groaned in a way that Emma didn't like, then slowly inched along its customary path.

When it was halfway free of its guard post, Emma marveled.

It was hiding a dumbwaiter.

Now *this* was the real story in the house. Glancing one more time over her shoulder, then studying the size of the dumbwaiter, Emma told herself that if she could fit in the basement window she could fit in this little thing.

And by God, she did.

It was a tight fit and pretty nerve-wracking— even her slight weight made the dumbwaiter shift ominously as she contorted herself into the little box—but once she was sure the mechanism seemed willing to accept her aboard, she tried the pulley rope within.

Soon, with a little experimentation, Emma lowered herself down the walls of the Smith murder house.

It only occurred to her about halfway to her destination that if she could fit in here, a child certainly could.

Who knew what else?

Light once again flooded the dumbwaiter. Emma peered cautiously through the opening before lowering herself all the way. It wouldn't do to go through such trouble only to be surprised as soon as she squeezed out of the dumbwaiter, after all.

And though she didn't see the Easter Ripper on the other side, the rabbits she saw were somehow no less startling.

Mouth open in shock, Emma twisted out of the dumbwaiter to examine the cramped hallway around her.

"Claustrophobic" didn't begin to cover it. "Psychotic" came closer. Emma had speculated that the person leaving the note was only trying to emulate the handwriting of the insane, but maybe she was wrong about that.

The rabbit murals on the walls seemed a strong argument in favor of disorganized mental illness.

Bunnies, bunnies, bunnies. Everywhere she looked. Every wall of the cramped, L-shaped hallway was ornamented with elaborate springtime murals of Easter bunnies. It seemed Emma had stumbled into some perverse temple to the chocolate-giving holiday rabbit.

She struggled to convince herself that their beady black eyes didn't follow her down the hall.

And, as Emma tried the first door—locked, of course—that was the thought that inspired the cold, horrible truth.

The Smith house must have been full of crawlspaces like these.

All day, the whole time the Channel 9 crew had spent on-site, the Ripper must have been in the walls.

Watching.

Waiting with bated breath for the right moment.

Emma calmed her breathing as best as she could, ignoring the baleful stares of the rabbits around her.

Hurrying away from the locked door, Emma took stock of the other two and gave them both a try.

One opened to that final, nearly fatal room of the basement, which frightened Emma to look upon. As soon as she was oriented she shut the door, having paled just to see it.

The next door, however, was so much worse.

Emma had been prepared to find a few pieces of evidence attesting to the strange or perverse nature of the killer on which her team was there to report. She had not been anticipating any form of human remains.

It seemed to her that the cops ought to have found all that stuff by now, but as she stared in shock at the cold-mummified corpses around the room, the press on the subject came rushing back.

Most of the Easter Ripper's victims were never found.

No wonder. All the time they had been down here, their flesh being picked away by flies and rats to leave husks that were more skeleton than cadaver.

Tears filled Emma's eyes as she slowly pieced together the lurid positions in which these withered children had been shackled at death. One lay with its hands still over its face; another was profanely abandoned upon a bed; another, an infant or a toddler, had very clearly died in its crib of starvation. Maybe exposure. Who could tell these things?

Emma's fingers trembled.

The electric chair was too kind for the bastard.

All the more desperate to find Gary and get out of there, Emma turned around to leave.

Instead, she leapt in place.

A little blonde girl with a red mouth stood in the doorway, her large eyes fixed on Emma.

"Oh my God"—Emma stepped forward, lowering

the crowbar to show she was no threat—"are you okay? Did he kidnap you? I can't believe you're—"

The redness that Emma had briefly mistaken for smudged lipstick had gathered to maximum capacity. It now oozed down to the edges of the girl's jaw, where the thick red drops of blood slid down to meet one another at the delicate 'v' of her chin.

Emma stepped back while the bleeding phantom stepped forward.

"Stop," Emma pleaded, bumping into the crib and glancing over her shoulder with a wince of pain to have disrupted the dead in this room. As she whipped her head back toward the approaching spirit to find it far closer than it should have been, Emma clasped her hands and said, "Please, don't hurt me. He hurt my friends, too. I just want to *leave* this place—I'm a victim, too."

The girl's mouth opened.

The two streams of blood expanded into an unbroken curtain.

Her small hand touched Emma's clasped ones.

12

THE WALL WAS crying again. Two voices this time: sometimes it was just one or the other.

Like always when the wall was crying, Cassidy sat with her back to it and tried to make sense of the ugly sounds.

The strangest thing about the crying walls was that they sounded like adults.

Did the Easter Bunny bring them to this place, too? Did it keep them here and do bad things to them? Would it ever let them go home?

Sometimes it was hard to tell if the walls were crying, or if some other kid was crying in another room, or if the Easter Bunny was crying. That last one happened sometimes, and it was the scariest.

Sometimes it was Cassidy who was crying, but less and less often these days.

Cassidy didn't have much energy to cry.

The Easter Bunny didn't feed them very often. If there had been a clock or a calendar or even just a window somewhere in the room, Cassidy would have been able to figure out how long it had been since she and the other kids locked in with her had been given so much as a scrap. With nothing but the four walls and the decreasingly frequent wails of the toddler who had recently been placed with them, there was just no way to know the lengths of time between their meagre meals.

Cassidy folded her arms around herself and lay down on the floor. The weeping in the walls grew more frantic, more desperate, then faded altogether. As if the very peak somehow inspired some profound realization of the futility of grief.

At a mere ten years old, Cassidy was coming to terms with that more and more.

She thought of her parents often. There was no doubt that they missed her terribly and were afraid for her life. She was afraid for it, too. All the same, thinking of her parents and their love was gradually becoming more painful than it was comforting.

In the early days of her imprisonment (for she wasn't sure as to the precise length of time, but she knew it had been at least a month), she'd fallen asleep each night enrobed in fantastic self-assurances that, any day, her parents and the police would come busting down the door. There would be nothing to worry about ever again, and the Easter Bunny would never hurt another child.

But the days wore on. The nights, too. Gradually, it

became more and more apparent to Cassidy that no one was ever going to come for her. Not the police, not her parents. Not even some fantastical guardian angel.

No.

It was just her, the Easter Bunny, and whatever other victims he deigned to put in with her.

At the moment, not including the baby, there were two boys and another girl. That was just in her squalid little cell, which smelled nightmarishly foul due to the bucket of excrement tucked into a corner. In other rooms of that evil prison, who knew? There could have been hundreds of children whisked away from their families. It certainly sounded that way on some nights.

This night, however, as the mysterious weeping faded, Cassidy folded her arms around herself. She nestled closer against the wall, as though it might do the job of keeping her warm in the absence of any kind of blanket, and found that the makeshift jail was unusually quiet.

On the one hand, this quiet was unnerving...on the other, she was just grateful to have room in her head for her own thoughts, or no thoughts. It was so good to close one's eyes and lie still, all the senses swallowed by the sweet relief and the warm, weighted sheet of fatigue.

Without food, exercise or sunshine, Cassidy seemed tired all the time. Her bones were too heavy to sit up. The richness of sleep was the one pleasure the girl still had left to her.

Her parents crept into her mind again as she fell asleep, which was the time she could not avoid them.

What would they think if she never came home?

She hoped they didn't think she had run away. She loved them. Cassidy would never have left home of her own volition.

Certainly not to come to a place like this.

The noise disturbed her slumber soon after she began to doze, but Cassidy knew better than to move so much as a muscle. Her body stiffened and her eyes remained shut while the door to the room swung slowly open.

Heavy, deliberate steps made their way to the center.

Something was set upon the floor.

The steps receded again.

Only when the door was shut did Cassidy open her eyes.

The basket of chocolate eggs sitting in the center of the floor made her mouth water on sight.

Cassidy sprang up, rushing toward the contrivance of brightly colored wicker and cotton-candy pink straw while saying to her cellmates, "Wake up! Wake up, there's food!"

The boys snapped awake at once, the girl stirring a bit slower and sitting up to rub her eye. "What is it?"

"Chocolate eggs," said Cassidy eagerly, snatching one from the basket. Its purple foil wrapping shone in the dim, never-off light of the room as Cassidy savored the sight, the heft, the scent.

Of course! The Easter Bunny couldn't be all bad, after all. Maybe Cassidy was just here because of something she had done. Soon she would get to go home, after all. This egg was a sign of that.

While Cassidy set to work peeling back the foil of a chocolate egg the size of her palm, one of the boys snatched another egg from the basket and nearly bit into it without removing the wrapper. He seemed to remember at the last second only because he glimpsed Cassidy unwrapping hers; then, embarrassed, he took the time to find a seam and unpeel the colorful foil.

The other girl looked warily at the basket, edging toward it but not yet taking anything it offered.

"We should be careful about these."

"He's not giving us any other food," said Cassidy with a miserable look at the chocolate in her hand. "Maybe he's trying to be nice."

"I don't think this is a nice Easter Bunny," answered the other girl, reiterating what they all knew too well already.

Frowning, Cassidy nodded but said nothing aloud. She merely turned the egg over in her hands, admiring the shine of its milk chocolate surface and investigating the strange lines cracking it throughout. Some kind of special filling, maybe...Cassidy's stomach rumbled with desperation.

Despite her hunger, she took only the barest scrape of chocolate from the end of the egg—just to taste it and make sure she didn't drop dead of some kind of poison right away.

The richness of the chocolate exploded across Cassidy's palate, a rich tsunami of nostalgic delight.

The girl exclaimed in joy, sighing much as the boys did while munching away on their own chocolate eggs. Seeing their happiness, the other girl looked anxiously at the basket but could no longer resist. She selected a green foil egg and studied it with reluctance.

"Oh, gosh, this stuff really is *good*." Cassidy peeled back more of her purple foil and lifted the chocolate to her lips again. "I've been so hungry!"

And then, Cassidy took her second bite.

Everything around her shattered into a shock of pain that tore through the roof of her mouth and the flesh of her tongue. The girl cried out, shock pulsing through her while she flung the bloody chocolate egg down upon the floor. The razorblade protruding from its surface bore the ruby stains of her blood.

The walls began to laugh.

"Are you okay?"

The other girl dropped her egg and clutched Cassidy's hand, her eyes wild and her pupils tiny with fear as they flickered toward the cackling walls. While blood poured from Cassidy's mouth, her cellmate wiped it away with a dirty hand. As the baby took to wailing, the girl implored, "Don't cry so much, try not to cry so much—look, when you wiggle your tongue it bleeds a lot, you're bleeding a lot—"

"Why is this happening to us?" Pitifully sobbing, Cassidy buried her face in her hands and drew back to her spot against the wall. "Why, why?"

The other girl shook her head, her face taut with a sorrow well in advance of any of their ages. "I don't know."

With a morose glance between the two of them, the boys studied the eggs they had been savaging to no apparent ill effect. Carefully, each tore his egg open and each, upon inspection, seemed satisfied that said eggs did not contain further razorblades.

Therefore, while Cassidy wept, blood overflowing her burning mouth the way tears overflowed her eyes, the boys made short work of the rest of their chocolate eggs. They then split the abandoned green one between the two of them.

While the younger boy studied his portion of the

egg with a greedy but nervous air and the older one chowed down without a second thought, Cassidy continued heaving sobs against the terrible agony—and, more than that, the injustice.

This wasn't fair. This wasn't right. It was *cruel*. She was just so hungry! She was just so hungry, and all she wanted to do was live a little longer. All she wanted to do was go home and see her parents.

While Cassidy sobbed, the wall laughed and groaned and cried with her. The towering bunny emblazoned upon it stared endlessly at her, its black eye fixed on her suffering.

The calmer girl patted her, soothing Cassidy and smoothing her blonde hair back from her face. "What's your name? My name is Jackie."

Cassidy tried to move her tongue, but more blood flowed out. Instead, she just hiccupped and shut her eyes for a miserable second of frustration. The younger boy's brow furrowed, a partial chocolate egg still held in his hand. The older boy, meanwhile, chewed his slower now, leaning back against the wall and looking as though he were lost in thought.

Scooting closer, the young boy said, "I'm Randy."

When he offered the chocolate and Cassidy shook her head, Jackie extended her hand.

"I'll take it," she said, adding with a glance at Cassidy, "if you really don't want it."

Cassidy nodded. Jackie smiled and, taking the chocolate from Randy, nibbled delicately on it. Her dark-ringed eyes shifted toward the older boy as she asked, "And who are—"

Jackie cut herself off with her own burst of laughter, her mouth still full of a bite of chocolate. The surprising noise made the starving infant produce once last fuss before muttering itself into quiet.

"Why," exclaimed the girl in the first bit of real mirth that had graced the room in days, if not ever, "he's fallen *asleep*!"

Randy laughed at that.

Even Cassidy tried to smile.

Soon enough, though, having taken the last two bites of her chocolate, Jackie's laughter faded into a look of terrible understanding. Her pale features grew all the more ashen at the sight of the chocolate on her hands.

Jackie turned her eyes toward Randy.

"Are you tired, too?"

"Uh-huh," Randy confessed, nodding his head. "I think I'm gonna go back to sleep…I was having a nice dream. My parents came, and—"

The boy's lips tensed momentarily, but his eyes had begun to grow heavy and did not match the affect.

"Anyway," he said, seeking out his usual corner and tucking his arms around himself, "good night again."

Randy's eyes were shut so fast that he didn't see the tears crawling down Jackie's cheeks. Mute with her mouth of blood, Cassidy took her turn patting the other girl. She didn't understand exactly why Jackie was crying until, with a glance at the staring rabbit on the wall, Jackie leaned in and whispered in Cassidy's ear.

"The eggs make us sleepy," whispered Jackie, her voice heavy with comprehension. "He put something bad in them. I'm getting tired, too…I didn't even have as much chocolate as them."

Cassidy's face grew cold with the draining of blood from her tearstained cheeks.

Was she going to fall asleep, too?

What would happen if she did?

Except, well—she didn't *eat* any of her egg.

Maybe, for some reason, she wasn't supposed to.

Softly talking to Cassidy about her home life to keep them both calm, Jackie began to doze off and Cassidy found herself obsessing over the meaning of what had just transpired. A basket of chocolate eggs, enough for all the older children to have one of their own.

Four eggs, four kids.

Three drugged, one trapped.

But why?

What did it mean?

She thought of the phrase 'drawing straws,' which she had never fully understood because it was from long before her time. There wasn't much use for the term in a literal sense these days, but she had heard it referred to in cartoons. She understood that it meant people sometimes needed to decide things at random, and in that case they would select from a series of items and see which one was the so-called lucky one.

'Drawing the short straw.' That was what her father called it when he had to do something at work that nobody liked.

Cassidy had drawn the bloody egg.

She just didn't know what it meant.

Not until Jackie was all the way asleep.

Not until the rabbit stopped looking.

Not until, while Cassidy sat awake from the pain of her bleeding mouth amid the sleeping bodies of her coevals, the door to their little cell opened.

Only then did she understand what it meant.

And she tried not to cry, because, somehow, she knew that he liked it.

13

EMMA LEAPT BACK from the specter as soon as its cold hands fit against hers. She cried out—

And by the time the cry was finished, the little ghost was gone.

It was not the ghost itself that had scared her, but its sudden appearance. Now that it had vanished and all Emma had left to prove the experience was her fast-racing heart, she felt a strange swell of guilt.

That ghost hadn't been a poltergeist, or some hideous phantom. It had been a little girl. A hurt little girl, who had suffered as few beings on the planet had ever been forced to suffer.

That was nothing to be afraid of, but everything to mourn.

"I'm sorry," said Emma to the vanished child. "I'm so sorry."

The spirits of the dead offered no response—but, for the first time in her deeply unspiritual life, Emma felt a connection to a world that was not the one she saw and felt.

Something was happening in this house.

Was the Ripper part of the same paranormal manifestation that permitted these children to appear in the corner of the eye or even touch a living human being? Emma was still not sure what to make of the killer currently on the loose. She would not be able to make up her mind without more evidence pointing to one explanation or another.

But that child had touched her.

That spirit had wanted her to know that it was at least real enough to be tangibly perceived. It had wanted her to see more than mere skeletons. It had wanted her to see a girl.

It had wanted Emma to share its thirst for revenge.

"Don't worry," Emma told the skeletons—no, the dead children around her. "I won't let the bastard get away with this."

Moving as quietly as she could, as though she were in a church or a tomb, (and in some ways the rabbit-decorated room was a little of both), Emma slipped into the hall and shut the door behind her.

Rabbits stared at her from within their bright, happy fields full of flowers and eggs.

She smashed her crowbar through the plaster of the nearest, caving in its face like the faces of the mother and brother in the Ripper's family photos.

Anger vented for now, Emma studied her options.

Aside from the door to the basement and the most apparent entrance to the tombs, there was only that sealed passage.

Now, *this* door...this was a heavy, promising sort of exterior door, though it didn't show any signs of giving at the pry of the crowbar. It was probably shut by some mechanism...probably one that had to do with that so-called Easter egg hunt.

Making a mental note of it for later, Emma lingered in the hall only to check the chest of drawers at the end.

Disgusting. Her nose wrinkled to find the perverse items within. Emma tried her best not to look at them, but it was very hard not to notice the medical equipment interspersed with...recreational items. It made her nauseous to think about, and she resolved to check only one last drawer in the vile container.

And boy, was she glad she did.

The box of shotgun shells rattled conspiratorially in the opened drawer. Her mouth opened and she looked rapidly around as though for some bomb to go off—but no trap was triggered.

Only her imagination.

Shotgun shells meant a shotgun was around here somewhere. Where, exactly?

She had no idea, but she was more than happy to stuff her pockets with as many shells as she could carry—eight bulky pills of buckshot, it turned out—and cross her fingers that she would have an opportunity to put them to use.

Between the phantom and the promise of a shotgun, Emma suddenly had a new drive to survive.

And somehow, so long as she kept fighting with all she had, she felt her survival to be in some way ordained. It were as though she had been anointed by the little specter who reached out to her.

She was ready and willing to kill the Ripper if that

was what it took to preserve her own life and avenge those of the dead.

And that was why Gary should have considered himself lucky Emma didn't bash his brains in when she opened the door to the basement and found herself face-to-face with her wide, pink boss whose tracksuit made her wince and remember Dana's murder.

"Emma!"

Now he remembered her name.

Emma relaxed the slightly raised crowbar and exhaled, telling him, "I've never been so glad to see you."

"The feeling's mutual. Dana's dead!"

Though her reflex was to try not to roll her eyes, Emma quickly overcame that and let him see her disdain. "I know," she told him witheringly. "I watched her die. Because I answered her screams, I was there. Where were *you*?"

"Wh—who? Uh, me?"

His pudgy fingers tented and drummed together while Emma tapped him in the chest with the crowbar.

"Yeah, you! Where were you? I heard her screaming all the way out in the yard—*you* were in here! You could have done something."

"I, uh, I was checking out the backyard for—"

"You liar! The back door is sealed."

"Okay," said Gary with a humiliated wave of both hands, which he quickly thereafter took to wringing. "Okay, I was—hiding."

"Where?"

Gary's lips trembled and he looked sheepish. Emma smacked his chest with the crowbar a little harder and demanded again, "Where were you *hiding*, Gary?"

"In the refrigerator," sobbed the producer, leaving Emma red in the face. "I took out the shelves and crammed myself in. God only knows how I fit…"

"So you heard *me*, too, huh?"

Gary said nothing.

Emma swore she felt a blood vessel burst in her head.

What a loser! What a coward! What kind of jerk hears two people screaming after a third has disappeared and *hides?*

This was the guy that Emma was trying to rescue?

She stayed *behind* for him?

So much for that. She should have hopped the gate.

Teeth grit, Emma shoved past him and made to storm out of the basement. To her horror, the greasy tyrant grabbed her forearm and said, "Say, Emma—now that we're here, how about we work together? I don't have a weapon—"

"Then you're just going to get me killed, if you haven't already."

"—but I have this," he said, coming out of his shame enough to look annoyed that his (former) intern was speaking to him this way. Emma paused to give him the benefit of the doubt. Beneath her tight expression, Gary patted down his pockets before producing a small iron key.

"What's that for?"

"Beats me." Gary shrugged and turned it over in his fingers. No identifying marks adorned it, so far as Emma could see. "Doesn't go to the front or the back door. There were a lot of locked rooms upstairs when I checked earlier, so maybe it's to one of those. We could find out together, if you'd just be willing to work with me here. Maybe if we get out I'll even give you a *real* job, huh? Not like Dana's gonna be much good to us anymore."

At the moment, Emma could not have given less of a fig about her dreams of being a journalist. Her only thought was of escaping this house in one piece and thereby still managing to *have* dreams.

But, if she was going to find a way out of here, she was going to have to try every option presented.

"All right," she said, "but I get to hold the key."

Gary almost laughed, closing it in his palm to hide it from sight. "That's some demand! Why should I trust you not to run off with it?"

"Because I'm a human being, and you're a human being, and no human being should ever be comfortable with letting another human being get killed?"

"I guess if you want to split hairs," said Gary tersely, "but human beings still have self-interest."

"Yeah, and I'm interested in the fact that if you get killed while the two of us are moving through the house together, you'll have the key in your pocket! Then what am I supposed to do?"

Lips pursing, Gary glanced back down at his palm. The gross, greasy glint he got when he thought he had a good idea sparkled through his shades. He looked up at Emma with a stroke of his moustache.

"All right," said Gary, "I'll let you carry the key—but you have to trade me that crowbar."

For a few seconds, Emma was totally taken aback by the absurdity of the proposal.

Then she remembered the shotgun shells in her pockets.

This was one hell of a gamble...but if that key turned out to be useful, it might very well pay off.

"Okay," said Emma after a moment of contemplation, extending the crowbar and an empty palm. "Trade on three?"

"Sounds good. One...two..."

On 'Three,' Gary dropped the key in her hand and snatched the crowbar. She let him have it, surprised and a little impressed in this case he was as good as his word.

"All right," he said, saying again after a few seconds of hefting the crowbar, "all right, yeah, hey, all right... now, how about that flashlight?"

Emma glanced up at him after stuffing the key in her pocket. "Excuse me?"

"I'm your boss, and the guy with the crowbar, and I want your flashlight."

"What a classy dude you are, Gary. Are you really saying you're going to hit me with that crowbar I just gave you if I don't give up my flashlight?"

Gary's jaw tightened and his hands twisted into pale fists around the crowbar.

"Look," he began, "I *gave* you the key—"

Something scraped along the stone wall near the basement steps a few rooms away.

Gary paled.

"The flashlight," he hissed.

Rolling her eyes, regarding him for a few cold seconds as the heavy steps announced the approach of the Ripper, Emma tore the flashlight from her shirt and tossed it into her boss's unready hands.

"Enjoy," she said. "I quit."

"What? But Emma—"

The Ripper's costume filled the farthest doorway, his bloodstained sickle at rest by his side.

"You heard me," Emma told Gary, yanking open the same door she'd just exited. "I'm through with

Channel 9, and I'm through with fetching coffee, and I'm through with *you*, *Gary*. No way am I letting you put my life at risk so you can feel safer...you're probably just hoping to use me as a human shield when you get a chance."

The Ripper raised his sickle and made his approach. In as stupid a decision as anyone had ever made, Gary grabbed Emma's shoulder.

"But wait, Emma! We need you! *I* need you! Your contributions to Channel 9 are essential!"

"Then you should have paid me like I'm essential," she told him, jerking her shoulder out of his meaty hand and hurrying to the dumbwaiter. While she folded herself into it as the fat man never could, she called to him, "But between you and me...no amount of money is enough to deal with this."

"Emma! Emma, don't be like that—how the hell do you *fit* in that thing—"

Gary had rushed down the hall to talk to her, but she was already tugging on the pully. The dumbwaiter responded with a jerk toward the second floor.

Emma looked her old boss coldly in the eye and gave him the finger.

"Have fun with your crowbar," she told him as she disappeared into the walls of the murder house.

14

THAT UNGRATEFUL BITCH!

This was exactly the problem with kids these days—these snotty 'Gen Xers.' You gave the little shits a chance to get their foot in the door of a major, established news network, and how did they thank you?

When the going got tough, they left you to die.

Spoiled, lazy, rotten brats. No interest in working anymore; no interest in pulling their own weight.

As Emma disappeared, was that fire in Gary's chest rage, heartburn, or a little of both?

That screwed-up rabbit was getting closer all the time. Gary was cornered. No way was he going to fit in that little box of a dumbwaiter, for starters.

Then, there was this hallway. His tendency had

always been toward claustrophobia, but this narrow little corridor seemed to have been built into the house by an amateur with no conception of standard ceiling heights. Don't even get Gary started on the murals...those rabbits were almost creepier than the one with the sickle.

Almost.

One of them was missing part of a face, though; and either it was his imagination, or something was wrong with the wall behind.

Was that the wood of a door?

Ah! Aha! Of course. No crazy guy could paint like this.

These weren't murals on plaster we were talking about...these were *wallpaper.*

Thrilled, Gary jammed his crowbar into the paper and yanked. A big crevice formed and he tore it wider, pulling strips away with sweaty hands made sticky by old glue.

Soon he uncovered the hole that had once been a doorknob.

Gary plunged a finger in to manually operate the mechanism, feeling around against the old brass workings until they gave way and the door swung into the room.

Just as the rabbit appeared at the hall's end, its heavy breathing audible, Gary leapt through the door and bisected about three feet of wallpaper rabbit to do it.

The skeletons on the other side made him wish he hadn't been quite so clever.

Chained by their ankles and necks or almost mummified with rope, the bodies were everywhere across the lightly furnished room.

This was his torture chamber, no doubt about it. Gary grimaced to see the way the kids had died but tried not to look too closely at everything around him...and he certainly didn't want to hang around disturbing the corpses.

But small and horrific though it was, this room had just enough space for Gary to evade the Ripper and get back out via the little hallway.

Trembling, Gary backed into the corner nearest the door, climbing upon a mattress with a skeleton to do it. He held the crowbar to his chest and waited, wondering how he would manage this.

With relentless patience, the Ripper's rabbit head leaned into the room to fix its black eyes on Gary.

Gary swallowed tightly and waved the crowbar.

"You want some of this, pal? Huh? Come on, come and get it. I'll smash them floppy ears in and take a gander at who's really wearing this get-up before I tell it to the cops."

The rabbit—the Ripper—stared.

Its empty black eyes remained dull, even with the flashlight shining directly on them.

As slowly as the rabbit had leaned into the room, so, too, did it withdraw.

Gary held his breath in anticipation for his pursuer to burst into the room and start swinging that sickle around.

His mouth was dry as that of the skeleton beside him. His fists went numb around the crowbar.

A door shut somewhere in the hall.

Astonished, Gary let his arms relax for just a few seconds.

What did this mean? Was this some kind of trap?

Whatever it was, he was grateful for the reprieve.

Palms sweating so vigorously he was worried the crowbar might slip from his grip, Gary sidled down from the thin mattress pad and edged toward the doorway. Carefully as he could, he examined the hall through the tattered hole.

"Empty," murmured Gary to himself, wrinkling his nose to slide his shades down and peer over their frame. Pushing them back up again, Gary crossed himself, kissed his hand like Nana used to, and carefully stepped out of the room.

The hallway was as quiet as a morgue.

Gary wasted no time. Wherever the rabbit was, it was likely planning to leap out and snatch him from one of these shut rooms.

With a warrior's cry, Gary lifted the crowbar over his head and charged through the hallway. Every step of the way, his body was braced for the murderer to leap out.

His scream only ended when he found himself in the basement and gasped for breath. Gary's head whipped around.

The rabbit was nowhere to be seen.

Though far from the most athletic sort, Gary pushed himself to move fast through the rest of the basement.

Much as in the hallway, he braced himself at every doorway for a big pink son of a heifer to leap out and take a slice at him.

And, much like in that creepy, rabbit-covered hallway, Gary was on the other side before he knew it.

Yes, there he was. Standing at the top of the stairs, feeling for the first time in an uncountable amount of minutes that he might actually make it through this thing alive.

Gasping, laughing, Gary pressed his hands together and waved them toward the ceiling. Then, his prayer short-lived, he whipped around in the kitchen and located the back door with a cry of relief.

Sure enough, just like that snotty intern had said, the door was sealed shut.

Didn't matter. Laughing to himself for his own cleverness, Gary tossed the crowbar lightly into the air. He caught it, twirled it, and hummed a few bars of "Puttin' on the Ritz" while slipping it between the door and the jamb.

Downstairs, the rabbit's blade scraped slowly along a brick.

"Good luck catching me once I'm in the woods, buddy," muttered Gary while applying pressure to the crowbar.

The rusted implement strained under the pressure.

Though Gary pushed, the door showed no sign of budging.

"Come on," he grunted, teeth clenched, "come on..."

Something popped in his spine. A vein bulged in his reddening forehead and he wheezed in pain, but he could not be stopped.

The producer threw every ounce of his impressive weight against the aged lever.

And the poor crowbar, rusted from years of neglect in the Smith family murder kitchen, snapped in Gary's hands.

Propelled by his own force, Gary collapsed against the wall and caught himself at the last possible second.

Swearing, kicking the wall and then the nearby garbage can, he shouted, "You sneaky little bitch! You tricked me!"

Yeah! That brat. It was all Emma's fault. He never

would have given her that key he found if he thought there were a chance of the crowbar breaking. Now he had nothing but a flashlight; nothing to defend himself from the killer whose footstep fell upon the lowest basement step.

Swearing to himself, Gary wheeled around to find a place to hide.

Instead, he almost tripped over the boxy white object on the floor.

Was that—

"Tom's camera," said Gary out loud.

The killer's steps broke into a sprint faster than Gary had yet heard it produce. He cried out, leaping into motion.

Too late.

Before it was even at the top of the stairs, the Ripper slashed out with the cruel hook of its weapon and tore open Gary's Achilles tendon. He cried out, leaping away, blood gushing from the back of his sock while he hopped through the kitchen.

When he stood in the doorway, the rabbit had made it to the top step and was raising its sickle to come after him.

"Help," cried Gary, "help—Emma! Emma, please, come back! I'll do anything! Help me! Just help me!"

The sounds of lighter footsteps echoed through the house upstairs.

Oh, thank God! Yes, Emma, yes! Maybe she wasn't such a selfish kid after all.

Gary stumbled forward, bouncing off pieces of furniture and almost tripping several more times as his slashed tendon made movement a struggle.

"Gary," cried Emma, her feet pounding on the stairs just as he made it to the foyer.

"Emma," he called, catching himself on the living room doorway and gasping for breath before pushing off to stumble toward her. "Emma, you gotta help me..."

Her scream alerted him to what was about to happen before it happened, but only just. Only with enough time for Gary to see the sickle slice down through the air for him.

Blood gushed from his shoulder as the blade sank into the meat of his torso.

An earthquake of pain too great to scream over ran through his dying body. It was too great to see through; too great to breathe through.

The tip of the sickle tore straight down through his sternum. Cut in half like a butchered cow from the side of his neck to the bottom of his belly while Emma screamed in horror on his behalf, Gary lurched forward.

His jaw fell open in astonishment.

The guts that tumbled out of him provided the bed for his landing.

15

EMMA HADN'T EXPECTED Gary to make it through the night without her, if she was being honest...but she didn't expect him to die so soon.

Certainly not right in front of her.

Leaving him behind was pretty awful. She felt bad about it just after it happened and the anger had slightly subsided, but the circumstances gave her no choice. She had been offered a way out—the dumbwaiter—and it just so happened it was one he couldn't take himself.

Besides, Gary had taken the crowbar *and* the flashlight from her. He had tools. She told herself he could take care of himself...though the thought never really sat right with her.

It seemed like a thought Gary himself would have had.

He had wanted to leave her disarmed; ready to throw to the wolves at any point in time that required it. Gary was a selfish man, and having a thought that even resembled one of his made Emma feel awful about herself.

But there was nothing for it. She was just going to have to hope he'd make it until she knew otherwise.

For now, coming to a stop in the attic, Emma unfolded from the dumbwaiter and grimaced at the new darkness of the attic. The flashlight hadn't done much, but it was a welcome addition to the bare bulb that only dimly marked the way to the door. The stairs were a little better and the hallway better still, but Emma turned that light off to avoid seeing Dana's headless corpse lying in an increasingly black stain.

Hands extended, Emma felt around the walls in search of the available doors. One was unlocked and contained an old bedroom where, reactivated by the restored power, a television buzzed with static.

Many other doors, however, were sealed shut.

One at a time, Emma tried the key.

The task was almost impossible in the dark—but only 'almost.' Used to navigating the world without her glasses in the early hours of the morning, Emma made her way down the hall detecting knobs by touch. Her hand would feel around and, upon finding the brass, her thumb would search for a keyhole.

Then it was a matter of trying the key.

In the first door, it wouldn't even fit.

The next door opened to a bedroom whose untouched state and still-made bed brought to mind the parlor downstairs. She shut it and moved on.

Another door after that was locked, and the key fit but wouldn't turn.

She was beginning to worry Gary had run a scam on her and presented her with some bogus key to a drawer or a cabinet when, at long last, it fit into the final door's lock with glass slipper perfection.

Holding her breath, Emma turned the knob until Gary's scream interrupted her.

The rest, as they said, was history.

Leaving the key in the lock, Emma dashed back down the dark hall and leapt over the area where Dana's body lay. She landed on that bad ankle and cringed.

If she had to flee the killer anytime soon she was going to have to think interms of hiding rather than running.

Then, on the stairs, she stood frozen as a statue while Gary's bisected torso sprayed a fresh coating of blood over the skull-like rabbit.

With a scream as the killer tore the sickle free of his newest victim and looked up at her, Emma turned to limp up the stairs.

The Ripper pursued her, moving faster than before.

Tears rolling down her face amid intrusive replays of Gary's death, Emma limped around the corner and hurried back to the room she had unlocked. Jerking the key from the knob, she slipped within.

A bathroom. She was in a bathroom.

Underwhelmed by the selection of hiding places, Emma settled right away on the clawfoot bathtub enclosed in opaque plastic.

She rushed over, yanking wide the shower curtain.

Emma only barely swallowed back her scream to find a dead man staring at her.

For a few seconds, Emma had no idea who this person was. His bowels were folded haphazardly upon his stomach and his hand was clenched in a fist over his shirt, the cotton fabric of which was soaked through with blood and vomit. His eyes bugged from his head in death and his mouth remained forever opened, shocked to a point of indignation that it was his time to die.

A floorboard creaked in the hallway.

Her stomach lurching to consider such a thing, Emma did what she had to in order to survive.

Her teeth grit, she pushed the man up by his shoulders and slid into the bathtub beneath him.

A door opened in the hall outside while Emma pulled the corpse over herself. He smelled like such a foul combination of organ meat and bodily waste that she worried she was going to be sick, but there was no other option.

The floorboards resumed announcing the movements of the killer.

While she waited with her eyes shut, it occurred to Emma whom this man must have been.

Jerry! The real estate agent.

Her brow furrowed. The poor guy! And Gary had been saying such rude things about him.

Just like she had been thinking such rude things about Gary.

It was a valuable lesson, Emma decided while the bathroom door slowly opened and the killer's footfall slapped upon the floor. Quietly as she could, Emma shrank beneath the body and smeared her face with the gummy substance of its dried blood to help her blend in.

In the future, (if she had a future), when Emma was stuck with a person she didn't like, she would exit the situation rather than stick around wishing the other person ill. You never knew what was going to happen to make you regret those thoughts...and life was too short to spend even a day at a place like Channel 9.

Emma saw that now.

As the rabbit pulled back the curtain of the shower, she shut her eyes and promised herself she'd never again waste time.

If she lived.

Emma held her breath and let the Ripper look where it would.

Seconds passed like minutes.

Slowly, the killer slid the curtain shut and turned to search elsewhere.

As the door shut, Emma exhaled slowly against the back of the realtor's head.

"Thanks, Jerry," she whispered, sliding out from under him just as soon as she could. Normally she would have waited in her hiding place to let her pursuer get out of hearing range...but she couldn't stand to linger.

Pulling herself from the tub with a grimace, Emma slid the real estate agent back into place and did what she could to shut his eyelids.

That worked a lot better in movies, it turned out. Wincing when his bugging eyes wouldn't shut, she instead searched her pockets and came up with a couple of quarters. The weight helped them stay... mostly shut, and it made her feel like she was engaging in a respectful exchange.

Because, well—she was going to have to search his pockets.

"Sorry about this," said Emma, grimacing while she patted the sides of his trousers.

The last thing she wanted to do was loot a dead

guy's body...but Jerry's car was sitting out there on the Smith property, in one piece and perfectly capable of getting her far away from this horrible house.

So, reluctant though she was, Emma forced herself to search for his keys.

And there they were, rattling in his right pocket during the pat-down.

Relieved, Emma fished them out. As she did, she bumped his hand.

An Easter egg rolled out across his blood-soaked chest.

Numb with astonishment to see the strange object fall from the dead man's fist, Emma reached into the tub and pulled out the egg.

For an Easter egg, it was oddly austere—and alarmingly precise.

Though most of the shell remained white, one side of it had been emblazoned with a perfect replica of the Justice tarot card.

But there was nothing just about any of this.

Emma would have smashed it if she hadn't needed it to escape—but as much as she despised what it represented, the discovery was better than any key.

Quietly as she could, Emma poked around the room until she discovered a bucket under the sink.

Trying not to think too hard about the brown substance lining its plastic surface, Emma placed the first egg inside.

So, this evil son of a bitch wanted an Easter egg hunt?

Then hunt, she would.

Emma cracked open the bathroom door and peeked down the hall.

The Ripper was nowhere to be seen, which made

her nervous but also presented an opportunity.

Her bad leg limping along as quickly as it could, Emma whisked down the hall, around the corner, and navigated carefully over Dana's corpse.

She paused before reaching the stairs.

Still quiet, Emma navigated back to the dead body cloaked in shadows.

Mouth dry, she flipped on the hall light.

If she hadn't spent so much time and effort trying not to look at the dead body of her coworker, Emma might have found the egg emblazoned with the Death card a whole lot sooner. Dana's red lips formed an 'o' around it, the features of her severed head slack and bloated in death like some kind of hideous display pillow.

"Sorry, Dana."

Wincing at the wetness of Dana's blood and frigid saliva while extricating it from her mouth, Emma shook the egg off, slipped it into the bucket with the other one, and wiped her fingers on her shorts.

"And thanks."

Leaving Dana where she was, Emma shut off the lights again.

Then, on her way down the stairs, she held her breath.

Of the two deaths, it was hard to tell whether Dana's or Gary's had been worse to behold...and the same was true of their desecrated corpses.

With the uncanny speed and strength of a beast in a nightmare, the Ripper had strung Gary up in the living room doorway using the dead producer's own belt.

The shoulder and half of the corpse's ribs accordioned out, this imbalance to weight causing

Gary to slowly twirl.

Emma grimly approached Gary's newly Y-shaped body.

Her stomach churned when she did not immediately see an egg in his hand or mouth.

Teeth clenched, eyes slitting closed so she might see as little of what she was about to do as possible, Emma stood before the dead piñata body of her old boss. She touched his side to keep him from spinning.

Trying not to puke as she did, she plunged her hand into the open cavity of his torso and felt around inside him. Her fingers tunneled past the meat of his back and into a still-warm stew of severed viscera and half-digested food. Although Emma gagged, her mouth hyper-salivating with disgust, she forced herself to keep going—to keep pawing around all the organs until she finally found it.

A cool, hard little shell amid all the wet guts.

Teeth clenched, Emma pulled it from the producer's body cavity and grimaced to shake it free of stringy red organ matter.

The Hanged Man stared back while Gary swayed placidly upon his belt, dripping blood that the recently departed killer had somehow managed to avoid tracking all around the house.

Was that it? Were these all the eggs? She had to hope so.

Emma had no weapon now. She was acutely aware of that fact while her gaze raked around the living room and her limping ankle slowed her path to the once-sealed parlor.

Now, however, the door stood open, the line of its wood pointing like an arrow toward Tom's camera in the center of the kitchen floor.

Emma's throat tightened.

Had Tom been somewhere around this place after all? With all the running around, she hadn't paid any attention to the location of his camera. Had he found it on his return and realized what was going on only too late?

For a few seconds after pulling the Hanged Man out of Gary's gut she had let herself believe that three would be all she needed.

Now, with the camera mocking her in the middle of the kitchen floor, Emma couldn't help but worry there was perhaps a nearly endless number of eggs. Was there one for every dead child, too? Would she have to go back to the basement?

Whatever the case, she had the distinct feeling that there was at least one more egg—and one more body—still left to find.

After setting the bucket on the kitchen counter, Emma stooped to grab the camera.

The Ripper snatched her up before she could even scream, lunging from the parlor like a snake from the brush.

Panic rang out in Emma's ears. She kicked wildly, slamming her feet back against the aggressor who struggled to restrain her arms. Emma smashed her skull back against the head of the costume, flailing, refusing to let him get both her arms along with the rest of her.

One arm slipped free and clutched the head of the costume.

Her fingers sank deep into plush fur.

If she was going to die, then she was going to die knowing who did this to her.

While the Ripper tried to snap her spine with or

without both her arms restrained, Emma yanked the head of the rabbit away from the rest of the costume. The dead-eyed face fell to the floor, rolling beside Tom's camera while Emma blindly thrust her thumb back into the Ripper's eye.

It took two tries. The first bounced off what felt like a cheekbone, but on the second stab her thumb jammed into something soft.

With a man's cry, the killer released her.

Emma scrambled forward. Thinking quick, she grabbed the head along with the camera.

By the time she turned around, both objects in her arms, the Ripper had retreated into the parlor.

The door slammed shut behind him.

Gasping for air, Emma darted through the living room, beyond the front hall and up the stairs with her new prizes. Halfway there, her ankle began to give her trouble. She slowed, forcing herself to limp along, her heart racing.

She'd done it. She'd unmasked him.

If he tried to kill her again, she'd get a chance to see who he really was.

Upstairs, Emma limped through the pool of Dana's blood in pursuit of the one television she had seen in the house. She dropped the rabbit's bloody head before, with trembling hands, she removed the tape from Tom's camera and turned it over in the dim light of the room.

Did she want to see this?

No.

But she needed to.

Emma slid the tape into the VHS player.

With her eyes fixed on the screen, she rewound the tape and leaned back to watch.

16

THE CAMERA PANNED across the living room of the Smith murder house. Its attached light did little to reduce the uncannily dark quality of the footage once Tom moved away from the studio lights.

"I don't know what's going on," Tom said to the camera and whomever would eventually find it, "but I just got back, and—everyone's gone. I think something's really wrong."

The camera zoomed in on Dana's shoes before focusing on the trail of her blood.

Tom gasped.

"Dana—"

The camera jostled violently as the man holding it launched into motion. Tom rushed up the stairs two at a time, but only made it three quarters of the way before the reporter's corpse came into frame, one arm extended and one shoulder red with the blood of a missing head.

Crying out, Tom zoomed in, then hurried up the stairs with a sob in his voice. "Dana! Dana, oh, Dana—oh, no—"

Another groan of mourning wracked through him. The camera zoomed in on Dana's head, keeping it in the shot for five long seconds.

"Dana," whispered Tom, "oh, Dana, I'm so sorry...how could this happen?"

The camera whipped around as Tom approached the dark bend of the hallway, but ultimately he drew back once again.

"I don't know what to do. I don't know what to do, oh, God help me! I don't know what to do."

The camera bouncing wildly with his faster stride, Tom hurried back down the stairs and swept through the living room. His footage illustrated Tom's next few minutes were spent quietly gasping to himself as he tried the knob of the back door, then checked the shutters of sealed windows.

A clatter rose from the kitchen.

Hyperventilating, Tom rushed to the little door under the stairs.

Cut to:

"I thought that was the killer," whispered Tom, pushing open the little door and leaning out to sweep the camera's lens across the hall, "but I think it actually might have been Gary...unless Gary is the killer. I guess it could be anybody except Dana—poor Dana."

Back through the living room, then the kitchen, Tom panned across the contents of the house and softly narrated.

"Best as I can tell, our story has disrupted some kind of—angry spirit. That, or a copycat killer is on the loose. I don't know what else it could be."

With a trembling hand, Tom opened the door to the parlor and explained to the camera, "I heard the Easter Ripper has a twin nobody knows about. That he's innocent, and he keeps to himself."

The camera zoomed in on a family portrait of a mother and two sons, with the mother and one of the boys missing their face. The black felt at the back of the frame showed through to give them a ghoulish, bone-chilling appearance.

"Which one is the evil one, I wond—"

Something crashed somewhere; near or far, it was impossible to tell.

Tom whipped around with the camera, calling, "Hello? Hello?"

No response. He backed up, scanning the room and zooming in on the door.

"Emma? Is that you?"

As though the tape were bad, the image shook with tracking problems. Tom uttered a cry even sharper than the one upon seeing Dana.

The camera whirled left and the tape managed to rectify its quality just as a boy in a red baseball cap vanished through the shuttered window.

"Did you see that? Did you see that? I hope I got it—I know I saw that just now. I know that was real. I—oh, God—"

Without any obvious prompting, Tom rushed behind the plush red chair of the parlor. There he crouched, holding the camera for only a few seconds more. As his breath hitched with fear, he lowered it softly to the ground. Finally, with a gasp, he could be heard scrambling back.

"No! No, please—"

While Tom cried out, the abandoned camera accumulated unchanging footage of the old fireplace.

"Who is it? Who are you?"

No response.

"Stay back, I'm warning you!"

Tom could be heard scrambling back, but the killer was silent as ever.

"No," gasped Tom, desperation in his voice, "no, please, stop—no! No!"

His protests raised in an aborted scream of mortal agony that was nothing more than a gurgle before it took shape.

Silence filled the room.

The Easter Ripper slowly loomed into view and bent before the fireplace, where it slipped something behind the black grate.

Its blood-splattered pink belly and giant rabbit feet turned to face the camera.

Those feet, like pink clown shoes, slowly closed the distance.

The footage ended.

17

EMMA STOPPED THE tape.

That had to be where the last egg was hidden.

Not with the location of Tom's body, but at the site of his death.

Emma's lips pursed with her reluctance.

The parlor was where she had found the Ripper just now. Had Tom's death only occurred moments before, or had this all happened earlier? Was it just now being used as bait to trap Emma?

She rewound the footage enough to see a timestamp and nodded to herself. Yes, that was about when she was down in the secret area of the basement—when she was approached by the spirit of that dead girl.

Emma ran her hands over her face.

She was going to have to see another corpse.

And that was assuming she could get into the parlor at all. Had the Ripper left, or was he still lying in wait?

Seemed unfair for him to camp out where she was supposed to be putting the eggs. The words of his note echoed through her head.

Some game. Games were supposed to be fair.

There was nothing fair about anything the Easter Ripper did.

Even what he was doing to Emma's mind was unfair—although, between the ghosts and the death and the apparently resurrected killer on the loose, she still couldn't decide whether she was seeing things, or whether true paranormal events were happening.

All she knew was that, upon cracking open the door to the hallway, red light had filled the entire corridor.

Emma could not believe her eyes.

The red light that accompanied the premonition of death and now flooded the hallway before her was the most all-encompassing of all her strange visions in the house. Perhaps it was even the most frightening. It spilled in across the floor and left her hand looking like it was covered in blood.

She recoiled, reflexively checked herself, then leaned as cautiously as she could into the upstairs hall.

Her stomach sank.

The words "HELP ME" were written across every wall, and in that same disorganized handwriting from the note. It covered every inch of the wallpaper and ceiling, though it was difficult to read the text between the way it was clustered and the bright scarlet light that seemed to come from nowhere and everywhere at once.

Perhaps it came from the Ripper's head. The great black eyes of the pink rabbit stared at Emma as it barreled down the hall straight for her, nothing about it making sense. Her brain parsed the scuttling legs of a spider that carried the head toward her amid disembodied howls from voices that belonged to adults as well as children.

Screaming, Emma ducked back into the room and slammed the door before the horrific pseudo-spider could come close to her.

Sick to her stomach with fear, Emma stood with both hands on the knob she held shut.

After a few seconds of silence, she realized no more light poured in beneath the door.

Though she calmed, her eyes fell on the Ripper's true head. It sat crookedly on the floor, its floppy ears and matted fur resembling Dana's sagging flesh when separate from its body.

Unable to stand it, Emma grabbed it by one ear and shoved it into the television cabinet whose door she slammed shut.

Emma tried to control the chattering of her teeth while giving the doorknob another twist.

The door swung open into the empty hallway, where old floral wallpaper was untouched by anything but time and smears of blood.

Gasping with relief, Emma briefly buried her face in her hands and tried to regain some sense of direction. Her mind reeled. Was that something that had actually existed? Had she really seen that?

She wasn't sure if it was better or worse than losing her mind. Frankly, if this was all somehow in her head, maybe a doctor could help her. Maybe all of this would go away and she would never have to think of it again.

Then she turned the corner and saw Dana's body.

There was no escaping this reality.

Tears filled her eyes. This time, Emma made herself look. Having discovered the egg that way, as a gift to her from the dead, and having had these experiences of communing with the children whose spirits haunted this awful house, Emma felt she owed a new reverence to those who died so she could live.

And part of that reverence was witnessing their deaths—the awfulness of their deaths. It was carrying that awfulness inside of her forever so that someday, someone else might know at least a little of how much they had suffered. So that the torture they had undergone would not be in absolute vain, unknown and of no use to any living soul.

Accordingly, Emma made her slow way downstairs and studied Gary hanging in the doorway to the living room. The organs piled on the floor beneath him formed a little mound over which she carefully stepped, but she did not shy away from looking into the red cavity that opened before her, or the misery that lined her old boss's dead face.

How would Tom look when she found him? Emma's stomach tensed with the thought. She made her steady way through the living room, hyper-vigilant in case the Ripper should throw himself upon her at any moment.

Without his mask, though, he could not risk attacking her unless he knew for certain he could kill her.

Comforted but not lulled by the thought, Emma

slowed as she reached the kitchen. Gary's blood covered the floor. Was any of it Tom's?

Mouth dry, Emma considered the clutter on the counter but did not immediately see a knife. Even if there was one easily accessible, she had to wonder if it was really a good idea to use a weapon that required her to be so close.

The crowbar had been relatively good because it had a little bit of range. A knife? That was downright dangerous. One slash of the ripper's sickle and she would be disemboweled.

She had to leave her hands free in case she had to flee...but she hoped that she would be able to give him the eggs and go.

Such a possibility seemed unlikely. After seeing the chamber where he kept the tortured children, Emma couldn't help but suspect the Ripper was as crooked in his games as he was in his soul.

But, if she did her due diligence, she might find some bargaining chip—or, like the key that led her to Jerry, some new clue that would bring her closer to freedom.

Emma's every molecule seemed to vibrate with adrenaline as she sidled along the wall toward the shut parlor door. For a long stretch, Emma shut her eyes and listened for a sound that would give him away.

The singing of the sickle through the air.

The falling of a heavy rabbit's foot upon the floor.

The heavy breathing of the Ripper as he made his way through the house.

And she did hear it, that breathing.

She heard it coming up the basement steps.

Her jaw tense, Emma slipped quietly as she could

into the darkness of the parlor and crouched by the door to listen. Her hands pressed against it just in case he tried to open it, while her eye fit to the old-fashioned lock that made sealing herself in impossible without a key.

But she could peek out.

On the other side, the killer made his way through the shadows of the kitchen.

Peeping through a keyhole wasn't as easy as movies made it seem. Most of the image was cut off. She saw, in fact, hardly more than the usual pink blur of body as the Ripper stormed through the kitchen with the sickle in his paw.

There was little to see, maybe—but she saw enough. She saw that he was gone, off now to stalk through other wings of the house in the hunt for his quarry.

Emma had time.

And she needed it.

Most of all, she needed it to process what she was about to see. Still crouched by the door as she was, she had not yet endured the sight of Tom's corpse left abandoned on the floor. Whatever state it was bound to be in, Emma couldn't help but anticipate it would be the most awful body of all.

Steadying herself with a few seconds of shut eyes and a long, deep breaths, Emma turned around.

Amazingly, Tom's blood had not yet formed enough of a puddle to be apparent around the armchair; nor had his legs fallen into view when he collapsed on the floor.

Was he at some odd angle?

Emma made her slow way around the chair, her body braced for the horror of death.

And she found nothing.
No body.
No blood.

Disruption in the dust? Yes—but it was hard to tell without a flashlight exactly how disrupted it was.

Had the killer disposed of Tom in a bloodless fashion before carrying his corpse away somewhere? For what purpose? The egg was already hidden, wasn't it?

To check, Emma hurried to the fireplace and poked around beneath the uncleaned piles of ash.

Sure enough. Emma's hands closed around something smooth.

She drew the egg out of the ash and blew it clean. The tarot's Fool gazed back at her, smiling blissfully while about to take his first step off a cliff.

The egg really was there.

Why, then, move Tom's body anywhere?

Emma supposed that was like asking water why it was wet. Why did a child-murdering psychopath do anything? Why had this spirit, or perhaps this copycat killer, seen fit to prey on Channel 9's innocent team?

It was useless to try and guess anything. Emma was so far beyond asking questions that it was almost sad—an affront to her own sense that she was meant to be a journalist.

Maybe she was still meant for the role, but one thing was for certain…she wasn't going to ever be a war reporter. Who could ask questions and hope to get at the truth when their very life was at stake? Only the coldest of the stone cold could possibly think of reporting at a time like that.

Tom had done it, somehow. He had picked up the camera and filmed everything—even one of those ghost children.

The one frame of the child made Emma feel much less insane, but it left her with still more questions she just didn't have the energy to ponder.

Her limp more pronounced all the time, she made her way to the Easter basket and set the Fool egg into its colorful straw.

Something, some mechanism built into the base of the basket, clicked.

Nodding slowly, Emma slipped out of the room with a glance toward the rest of the house. She plucked the bucket of eggs quietly from the counter and bore it with her to the parlor.

There, one at a time, she set them all into the clicking Easter basket.

First, Dana's Death egg.

Click.

Then, Jerry's Justice egg.

Click.

Finally, with a particularly long look of regret, Emma nestled Gary's Hanged Man egg in against the other three.

Click.

That was it?

That was *it*?

Emma groaned.

"Don't tell me there are more eggs—four bodies, four eggs! Let me out, you bastard!"

The house provided her with no response.

Her chest tight, Emma ran her hands over her face and tried not to cry.

If she didn't find a way out soon, she was going to die.

There was no question about it. If there really were more eggs, sooner or later the Ripper was going to catch up with her. Emma would be done for.

She was just going to have to check around and hope she either found an egg, or a way out.

Throat tight with anxiety, Emma emerged in the kitchen.

Where in the house were there more bodies? Since corpses were where he kept the eggs, it might behoove her to find Tom's corpse, after all.

But—what about the children?

Emma listened to the house for a few long seconds before making her way in perfect silence down the basement steps.

The sight of the washer struck her as surreal, as did the small window before which something had been placed. Somehow it seemed like a thousand years had passed since she'd wiggled into this basement. A different person—a more unassuming and trusting person, for starters—had been the one to follow her boss's orders to break into this place and let them all in.

If only she'd quit right then! Better still—if only she'd never taken this terrible internship, or quit her first day on the job. Dana had stuck in there for years, biting her tongue and ignoring sexual harassment; Tom took constant abuse from management simply for being a quiet and introverted cameraman; even Gary had been put through the wringer by Channel 9, always chasing the dragon of the story that was finally going to make his career.

From the lowest of the low to the most prominent members of the station, every single person who slaved away at Channel 9 was getting the shaft.

This story, this evil night in the murder house—this was only the most absurd example.

The basement was empty of killers as Emma made her way through it, though it was also empty of anything useful. To her great frustration, the disorganized mess contained nothing with range. No gun, as had been promised by the shells in her pockets.

Evidently, she was going to have to settle for something up-close—or so she planned.

Palms sweating, Emma turned the knob to the den of horrors in the basement.

The door at the end of the hall stood slightly open.

Emma's heart leapt into double-time and she rushed to the end of the corridor, where she peeked around the corner to ensure the killer was out of sight. Satisfied, she wiped her hands off on her shorts and neared the heavy door.

She really *had* found all the Easter eggs.

Mouth dry, Emma pushed the gray door a little wider. It groaned open at her behest, pushing away like a curtain to reveal the fortified walls and ceiling of a tunnel carved beneath the property.

A noise that was as much a cry of joy as a gasp of relief burst from Emma's mouth. Brow furrowed, hands briefly clasped in gratitude, the former intern of Channel 9 dragged her bad ankle into the dark hall and shut the door behind her.

Where would this tunnel end up? The darkness was so complete that she had to run a hand along the earthen wall, her fingertips sometimes bashing into support beams installed to keep the roof from collapsing. Much like the secret section of the basement, the hall was dangerously narrow, and she couldn't help but think that if she met the Ripper in the dark she would be absolutely done for.

But she met nothing in the dark. No Ripper, no

spirits. Not even a bug that made her aware of its presence.

Instead, she found a ladder.

Her heart soared.

This was it! Yes, oh, this was it. Emma was going to be free. She'd come up out of this hatch somewhere on the grounds, find Jerry's car, start the ignition, and drive away.

How sweet that engine would sound! Emma smiled to herself while hurrying up the rungs of the ladder that, dangerous as it appeared, was nonetheless the happiest portent she had encountered in hours.

And like so many other things in the Smith house, it betrayed her.

The ladder that had seemed such a joyous sign released her not into freedom, but into the greenhouse.

Yes—the very same greenhouse where all those children were brought when it was time for them to die.

Emma's fingers trembled, her joy revealing itself to be its twin, despair, in thin disguise.

Was she going to die here? *Really*? Emma supposed that she had to accept it was a possibility. Denial wasn't going to help her in any way.

But accepting that death was a very real, very possible outcome of the hellish night—that did help Emma somehow, some way.

It made her all the more dedicated to kicking and clawing and screaming her way through to the end— to the moment when she would at last break free of this evil property and be alive, really alive, for maybe the first time ever in her life.

Out of this violence, this horror, Emma would find herself.

In fact, as she spotted the shotgun hanging on a rack of tools on the other side of the greenhouse, Emma realized she was finding herself more and more by the minute.

Yes, yes, yes, yes!

Here it was—here was what she'd been looking for all along. Here was the *real* key to victory. Forget locked doors and Easter egg hunts.

As Emma tore the pump-action shotgun down from the rack, she gave it the impulsive kiss she had only barely avoided giving the rusty crowbar.

Her fingers trembled as she loaded the weapon. The thing took one in the chamber and two in the loading tube. With an expert hand developed from years of hunting birds with her grandfather outside Monroe city limits, Emma slid the fore stock into place and shifted the remaining shells from her back pockets to her front ones.

By the time her trembling hands had accomplished the task, the Ripper's heavy breathing announced his ascent up the ladder.

"I've got a gun! I'll shoot!"

There was a pause in the breathing and the soft ringing of ladder rungs beneath the weight of human limbs.

Then, a man's soft and mocking laughter.

"Are you really going to kill *me*, Emma?"

Taken aback, her mind struggling to sort out what it had just heard, Emma lowered the shotgun a few degrees. Her brow furrowed.

"I know that voice," she said, far more to herself than to the killer approaching. "I know that—"

The Easter Ripper's bloodstained paw emerged from the chute and dragged out the rest of him.

Emma's hands trembled with confusion.

Tom used the sickle clutched in his matted fist to push himself up from the greenhouse floor.

18

TOM WATCHED FROM the corner while his mother tore his brother a new one, her finger wagging in his face and her eyes bright as fire.

"I thought I told you to share those chocolates!"

"But Mom—"

Anthony's watering eyes flicked desperately over at Tom. As always, they overflowed with the mistaken hope that this time would be the one when his twin would intervene and tell the truth.

Tom smiled, then let the expression drop so as not to be caught wearing it when their mother turned around.

"Don't *tell* me you were just about to blame your brother *again*, Anthony Smith. What is wrong with you?"

Their mother's hand rang sharply against Anthony's cheek and the tears exploded from him.

"I raised you *better* than that, young man. If you don't learn to take responsibility sometime, you're going to grow up and become a useless layabout. Worse, some kind of criminal. You'll go to prison. Do you want to go to prison, Anthony?"

The boy shook his head, tears rolling down his emotion-mottled cheeks while their mother nodded in approval.

"That's right. You want to stay *out* of prison and live a good, productive life—but you won't ever do that if you keep stealing and breaking things and blaming your brother for it."

Sighing, their mother regarded Anthony with a few seconds of pity before waving a hand that commanded Tom to respond. He did, slinking over and leaning into her arm as she said, "I wish you would try to be a little more like your brother, Anthony, that's all. Tommy didn't eat *your* chocolate, after all."

Tom shook his head earnestly, ignoring the dagger stare from Anthony's red-rimmed eyes.

"I'd never do that to you," Tom lied fluently, throwing in a wretched little sniff.

It was the sniff that put it all too over the top for Anthony. Stamping a foot and showing his indignation at the unfairness of it all, Anthony told their mother, "But I really didn't, Mom!"

Their mother's face tightened again. "That's enough, Anthony."

"He ate a whole bunch and—"

"Anthony."

"—and gave me a little so my breath would smell like it—"

"Anthony *Smith*, stop that at once—"

"—and then he went and brushed his teeth!"

"That's it."

Releasing Tom from her warm embrace, their mother caught Anthony by the wrist and showed no scrap of empathy for his desperate terror.

"Come on, boy," she said while dragging Anthony from the living room, "I'm going to have a word with you in my parlor."

While, pale with fear, Anthony attempted to pry himself from their mother's grip, he whipped his head around and locked eyes with Tom. Now Tom smiled again, full and wide and bright like a kid at an amusement park—though Tom had been to an amusement park once and didn't really see what the fuss was about, apart from the roller coasters.

Anthony had smiled, though. Smiled and laughed and at the end of the day cried when it was time to go home. Anthony made a lot of faces and expressed a lot of emotions that his twin just couldn't relate to.

While being dragged from the room to be beaten by their mother, though, Anthony's face adopted an expression that Tom *could* understand: rage.

'Mama's boy,' mouthed the older of the Smith twins as he was dragged from the room.

Tom's skull burned just to remember it all these years later. 'Mama's boy.' 'Sissy.' 'Butt-kisser.' Even standing in the greenhouse across from Emma, his ears rang and his face went red and his hand tightened around his sickle.

"You look surprised, Emma."

Her eyes were wild behind her big, round glasses, her mouth open in an 'o' of shock that reminded Tom of his mother when it was finally her time to die.

"It's you, Tom? *You're* the Easter Ripper?"

"That's right," he said coldly, "it's me. Quiet Tom. Unassuming Tom. Walk-all-over-him Tom."

His teeth clenched.

"Mama's boy Tom."

"But—but why? Why would you kill Dana and Gary? The real estate agent? Why copy the crimes of Anthony Smith?"

Tom's blood boiled with the insult. One paw of his true flesh rested upon his chest while, with the other, he gestured with the sickle. "Because! Anthony Smith was never the Easter Ripper—*I* was."

Emma fell back a step, levelling the empty shotgun with his chest. "What are you talking about? Wait, no—*you*. You were the brother!"

"Congratulations, Sherlock. That's right. Anthony and I were twins. My mother loved me and thought I could do no wrong...mostly because I was so good at making her think that. When something bad happened, she blamed Anthony and made him confess. It got to be second-nature for him. Any time I did something wrong, he took the blame."

"And when Randy Martinez escaped this greenhouse," said Emma with an unsubtle glance to the locked gate behind him, "Anthony went to the electric chair for you."

"Bingo."

"Then why kill any of us? Why Channel 9?"

"Isn't it obvious? For revenge."

Emma shook her head rapidly, now taking a single step toward him with the shotgun still aimed at his chest. Could she shoot that thing even if it *were* loaded? This was almost sad. No wonder she was an unpaid intern...not the brightest bulb in the drawer.

"Revenge doesn't have anything to do with it," she insisted.

"You don't think seeing my brother wrongly executed by the state deserves a little revenge?"

"No—and that's not why you're doing this, anyway."

Laughing darkly, Tom tapped his chin with the flat of the sickle. "Then you tell me, Dr. Emma...why am I doing this?"

"I think you're doing this," she said to him, looking him in the eye, "because you like it."

Tom shook his head and raised his paw to his face. Soon he was cackling, telling the ceiling, "What a genius! What a future she has in criminal psychology... that's right, Emma."

Tom lowered the sickle again and stared her dead in the face, letting her see the true emptiness inside of him play itself across his un-emoting face.

"That's right. I like it. I like killing. When Anthony went down, I thought I could control the urge to kill, because I had to—but now, it's back. And if it's back, so is the Easter Ripper."

Raising his sickle to savor the look of terror on her face, Tom advanced toward the girl.

He didn't want to kill her right away. She was so petite, so youthful, that she reminded him of the good old days. Maybe he could just incapacitate her and get her back downstairs. Then they'd have all the time in the world...and anyway, he needed to get some information out of her.

What had she done with his true head?

He might have asked the question aloud right then if Emma hadn't interrupted him by saying, "Stop!"

He laughed and kept coming.

Emma pulled the shotgun's trigger.

Tom was so shocked to be knocked back by a burst of buckshot that he wasn't exactly sure what had happened for a few seconds. Not before the burning began in his chest and his own red blood oozed through his fur.

Astonished, Tom laughed.

Emma's face was ringed by even greater terror than before. Maybe she had been expecting him to fall.

As she pumped the shotgun, Tom told her, "Say, Emma...that was pretty good."

As he drew the sickle back to take a wide swing, Emma uttered a cry and ducked between a row of planters.

He had been aware of her twisted ankle in the aftermath of the poodle incident, but even with that to consider, Emma's limp was *bad*. With all the chasing her around he'd been doing, he'd gotten her to put enough pressure on it that every few steps she just sort of dragged it along for a hop or two. Then she'd get it into motion again, darting forward a little before once again yielding to the pain.

He could use that pattern to his advantage if he could just catch her at the right time.

While Emma hurried down one row of planters, Tom followed her along the one adjacent. His costume hampered him, but between the spacing of his strides and his own undamaged legs, he reached the end of the planter at the same time she did, popping around the corner to slash first and aim later.

Emma screamed while the sickle snagged a portion of flesh that turned out to be an arm, but the shotgun blast she reflexively released knocked him and his sickle back a few feet before he could try to sever the limb. The dislodged blade produced another scream from his intended victim, who pumped the shotgun and spent another shell that hit him in the chest like a fireball.

Tom gasped, blood splattering out of his mouth at the pain. For a few seconds, he was dizzy.

Then, driven onward by the trembling in limbs that demanded they make themselves the instruments of death, Tom found his footing. He charged Emma.

The intern's eyes widened with her scream. She just barely ducked the subsequent swing of his sickle, narrowly squeezing past him and limping along the perimeter of the greenhouse. He saw exactly where she was going and let her go there.

Tom took his own, slower path around to meet her at the gate.

"Where'd you find those old shotgun shells? I thought that thing was empty...how many did you find, Emma?"

His own blood had turned almost all of his fur red by now. One paw upon his chest, Tom heaved a breath of painful air and found a new wind. He straightened up again and, driven forward as all predators are driven by their hunger, he made his way toward Emma's cry of despair. The locked gate rattled under her hands.

"Did you really think I'd just let you escape, Emma?"

A series of rustling and clicking noises drew him closer. As he appeared around a row of dead squash vines, Emma slid a shell into the gun's tube and swung it wildly up at him.

"Do you really think you can kill me?"

"I think this shotgun will do a good job of it," she said, firing off another shell.

This burst of pain was the worst of them all so far. Tom did not experience pain very often and so to feel it now, this hot explosion across his chest and face, he gasped. It was almost a surprise—almost exciting to think that he had made so many people, so many children, feel this way...or worse.

Certainly exciting to think of his mother making his brother feel that way—and all because she couldn't accept that her precious Tommy was rotten to the core.

"Is that all you've got?" Tom spat out a mouthful of blood and raised his sickle, lurching toward the girl who cried out and pumped the fore stock.

"Don't you get it, Emma? You're going to die here tonight. I'm going to kill—"

The next shell burst from Emma's weapon. She pumped it rapidly and fired off the next, and while Tom fell to his knees in a daze, Emma dug through the pockets of her shorts with a visibly shaking hand.

She'd shot this kind of gun before, it seemed.

Breath wheezing anxiously through her teeth as Tom climbed to his feet, Emma raised the weapon again.

One shell at a time, she fired.

19

EMMA SOBBED IN relief.

Tom careened forward beneath her final two shotgun shells.

How was this possible? Was he even human in the first place? She had spent *eight rounds* of ammunition on him and still was not sure he was dead. Tears streaming down her bloody face, Emma hurried forward and turned the gun around.

Raising it above her head, Emma smashed the shotgun down against Tom's skull once, twice, three times.

That was all she could stand.

She had to make sure he was dead, but she didn't want to.

This was *Tom*. This *was* Tom.

Tom was the Easter Ripper.

Her brain just couldn't grasp it. Even with everything fitting together as it did—even with the sense it made and the cold, hard evidence before and around and behind her—Emma struggled to make herself believe it.

Somehow, even though he had swung this sickle after her, had chased her down and slashed open her arm and tried to kill her or worse, Emma still stood there awash in horror to think she had murdered her own friend.

She stumbled back a few steps, her ankle shrieking with pain every step of the way. It was pushed to its limits. There was no more running for her.

Oh, God. He was dead, and Emma was glad he was dead—but was that right?

Was she a killer now, and all because she had killed Tom? Was she as selfish as Gary was because she had left him to die? Was she as deluded as Dana because she, too, had told herself that enduring the misery of Channel 9 was safer and therefore better than trying to excel somewhere else?

More and more as the night deepened, Emma found herself evaluating her own personality. Had she fallen asleep at the wheel? Maybe she had never even been awake at all. She didn't know.

She just knew that she looked around this greenhouse full of dead plants and overturned pots and long, rectangular planters that were barren from neglect; and then at her dead friend in his blood-soaked rabbit costume; and she decided that something had to change.

"Maybe I'll move away from Monroe," she said to herself, dropping the shotgun and stumbling toward the gate.

Yes, that was it. She'd go away—far away. Maybe a big city, or maybe just away. Out of the country. Now that would be an adventure!

She could do anything now. Yes, anything.

Looking another person in the eye again might take some time...but she'd get there.

Emma had done what she had to do. She had survived, and that was what mattered.

With quivering hands, Emma limped back toward the gate. When would the endorphins and dopamine and other wonderful chemicals rush through her brain? That would be any minute, right? She hoped so...she shook with adrenal fatigue, hyper-alert, exhausted to the core.

At the lock that had defied her exit and almost cost her life, Emma studied the knob and the plate around it. The key must have been somewhere in the house. Would she really have to go back in there? Maybe she should just break a window in this greenhouse and climb out...didn't want to cut herself on the glass, but anything sounded better than stepping foot inside that murder house ever again.

Emma bent to pick up a nearby brick from a discarded, spider-web covered pile.

When she straightened up, the Easter Ripper's body was nowhere to be seen.

Alarm bells sprang up in Emma's heart. She lunged toward the abandoned shotgun, all her reluctance to return to the house transmuting in a second to necessity—

And the Ripper grabbed her from behind as her bad ankle gave out beneath her, finally failing when she needed it most.

"Sh, Emma."

One bloody paw, matted with filth and organ-meat and who knew what else, slapped over her mouth while she cried out in pain. The other kept hold of both her arms along with her torso. She struggled in vain while he told her through teeth whose lips had been torn away by a shotgun blast, "You can't *kill me*, Emma."

His voice rose in a scream.

"I'm the Easter Ripper! Do you understand?"

He grabbed her face and turned it toward his, staring her down with a wild insanity that contained nothing—absolutely nothing.

"I *have* to do this," he whispered intensely, pulling her toward the center of the room. "It's what Anthony never understood. It's what Mother never understood. Eventually I had to keep *them* in the basement, too, or else she would have told the police. I didn't want to kill her, you understand? I *had* to kill her. She never would have gone along with Anthony, otherwise. Never."

Emma gagged at the wretched stench of the blood-soaked glove and tried not to let the wet breath of the Easter Ripper through tattered teeth make her panic.

"I loved her! She was good to me. I thought she would understand, but I was a fool. There's never been anybody who could understand me…there never will be. I'm alone. A mythical figure, apart from all mankind. The Easter Ripper. I'm going to live forever, Emma. Get it?"

At last, successfully wrenching her head out of his grip with a twist so fast and so hard she gave herself whiplash, Emma gasped. "But you're not, though! You're *not* the Easter Ripper, Tom. Don't you see?"

He stopped halfway across the greenhouse.

Still in his grip, Emma caught her breath while he belittled her.

"You still don't get it, do you? Even after I explained everything. *Anthony wasn't the Easter Ripper*. Get it, stupid?"

Whatever. Emma had heard worse from Gary. She didn't bat an eye. She didn't point out how stupid you had to be to be a murderer and not see the value of human love or human relationships. Emma used her training as an abused Channel 9 intern to internalize all the reactions that were the most natural. She simply told the evil man, "But your mask is off. I see you, Tom."

Emma looked up at Tom and stared him hard in the eye.

"While I see you without the head, you're not the Easter Ripper. You're not a mythic figure. You're a lame guy wearing a bunny costume. A nerd. A loser. That's it. Get it?"

His jaw tightened along with his arm, which squeezed Emma so tight she thought he might crack her arms against her ribs. While she cried out, she told him in defiance, "You can kill me right now, but you know it won't feel the same! You won't feel anything. Is that what you really want after tonight? You want the last kill from Channel 9—maybe your last kill ever, since it's all so high-profile—to be so exposed?"

"Where is it?"

His lack of lips flattened every word and sent a horrific admixture of blood and spittle flying from his teeth. Emma grimaced, her eyes shutting to keep the Ripper's bodily fluids from splattering across her field of vision.

"In the house."

"I *know* that, obviously. Where in the house?"

The Ripper turned Emma around in his arms and shook her with his paws on both her shoulders, demanding, "Tell me where it is or I'll *make* you tell me. Where's my head?"

"You're going to have to make me tell you," she said, her eyes burning with defiant fire.

Gritting his exposed teeth, the Ripper barked, "Fine," and dragged her along with him again, forcing her to cry out as she kept up on her failed ankle. "And I'm going to enjoy every second of it. You got into journalism because you wanted to get the real stories, right? Well, sister...I'm about to give you the inside scoop."

With one hand around her bleeding bicep to make her scream with pain, Tom leaned down to open the trap door of the greenhouse exit.

The tunnel wouldn't open.

"What is this."

A statement, not a question, muttered under his breath. Still holding onto Emma, Tom rattled the shut door to the ladder.

He looked sharply at her, demanding, "What did you do?"

"Nothing."

"Liar!"

The scream was almost inhuman. Tom rose, red-faced from more than just the blood, and gripped her face in his hands. "Tell me what you did! How did you lock that hatch?"

She hadn't done anything to it and didn't know how to respond, but the pressure he was putting on her skull seemed somehow very likely to smash her brains in. Tears welling in her eyes, Emma cried,

"How does it feel like I locked it?"

"I don't know."

Gritting his exposed teeth, his eyes—as soulless as the black eyes of the rabbit mask—burning with hatred, Tom searched Emma's face.

"It almost feels like someone is holding it shut."

Emma didn't know how to respond to that. It made no sense to her.

She could only cry out in pain and wait for death as shards of her skull burst into her brain. Emma shut her eyes, tears streaming down her cheeks.

And, with a noise of surprise, the Ripper released her.

While Emma fell to the ground, her throbbing head still in one piece, Tom stumbled toward the greenhouse door.

"What is this?"

Emma looked up, her bloodshot eyes struggling to make full sense of what she saw through glasses that had been twisted by the pressure of his grip. Struggling to adjust them on her face, Emma squinted in the same direction the Ripper wandered.

The boy in the yellow shirt stood before the greenhouse gate.

While Emma gasped, Tom looked the boy up and down and said with an expression of pure, malicious hatred, like a dog baring its teeth before a nasty dog fight, "You can't be here. I *killed you*."

The boy in the yellow shirt strode toward Tom.

Skeletal mouth opening in shock, a tattered piece of flesh flapping along his jaw at the wide movement, Tom whirled around to look incredulously at Emma. Instead he looked behind her and drew her gaze to a planter.

There, the girl with blood pouring from her mouth dragged herself out of the dirt.

"No," begged Tom, stumbling back down another row with a gasp. "No, no, no—"

Grimacing, Emma gripped the edge of the planter against which she'd fallen and used it to pull herself up. She recoiled when she looked down to find the corpse of an infant burrowed its way out of the dirt within like a legged worm.

All across the greenhouse, children of all sizes and shapes crawled from their graves.

Their number was greater than 11. Emma could not count them all because, as the Ripper shrieked, they clustered around their killer in a mob of death.

Their voices raised in screams of their own.

As they surrounded the Ripper, their screaming mouths sank into his flesh. Their hands tore away his costume to give them access to his body.

The withered form of his mother crawled through the victims to take her son's face in her long, branchlike fingers.

Tom's brow knit.

She leaned forward and bit off his nose, blood spurting from his nasal cavity to spray across her expression of rotten disdain.

As the Ripper released his last scream and the children climbed over one another to consume his evil flesh, a great white light glowed from the center of the throng.

Emma cried out.

When the light became too intense to bear, she raised her hand before her eyes and turned her face away.

PUPPET COMBO®

Influenced by slasher movies and low-poly survival horror titles from the PS1 and PS2 eras of gaming, Puppet Combo® is a prolific studio whose titles range from nightmarish offerings like POWER DRILL MASSACRE to the more conceptually surreal FEED ME, BILLY. Check out Puppet Combo®'s website for more on its games, including MURDER HOUSE—then, support the creation of new games (and get tons of fantastic content) by contributing to their Patreon.

REGINA WATTS

Regina Watts is an author of transgressive and splatter fiction, and a longtime fan of Puppet Combo®'s games. If you enjoyed this novelization, be sure to explore Regina's work on Amazon—especially her splatterpunk novel, MAYHEM AT THE MUSEUM. Get free stories by signing up for her newsletter, and don't be shy about leaving a nice Amazon review if you enjoyed MURDER HOUSE: it's an easy way to help both creators at the same time!

Made in the USA
Columbia, SC
30 November 2023